USA TODAY BESTSELLING AUTHOR

Dale Mayer

HEROES FOR HIRE

NORTH'S NIKKI: HEROES FOR HIRE, BOOK 15
Dale Mayer
Valley Publishing Ltd.

ISBN-13: 978-1-773360-90-4
Print Edition

Books in This Series:

About This Book

In what circumstance wouldn't a knight want to rescue a damsel in distress? A former SEAL working for Legendary Securities, North Dockter has found the very circumstance that challenges even his stalwart, chivalrous ways. Nikki Beckwith is a firecracker who butts heads with him at every turn, refusing to follow orders or listen to his experience unless doing so suits her.

When she discovers someone is smuggling drugs through her company's warehouse and her life is threatened, Nikki flees to her aging grandfather's home in England to lay low and regroup. He's always been there for her, and, if ever she needed a bolthole to make changes in her life, it's now. Maybe it's time to return to the States…particularly after meeting North and realizing the attraction between them is more than she believed possible.

But Nikki soon realizes that no place is safe after her grandfather is attacked in his home. Even with her gorgeous guardian angel hovering close by, will she be too late to make all the changes she's envisioned?

Sign up to be notified of all Dale's releases here!
https://smarturl.it/DaleNews

Prologue

NORTH DOCKTER WAS a sucker for a happy ending, which was good because Levi's compound was a bloody mess of sappy stories. With Liam having his very own Lily, he traveled back and forth to visit her at the elephant sanctuary when he had days off. Liam kept a room here at Levi's compound, where Lilianna was a regular visitor.

Her father, Jim, had stepped back into his world as if he'd never stepped out. And it appeared the sanctuary was thriving under his leadership once again. Press releases picked up his miraculous return to good health, and the funds poured back in again. North was proud of everybody's contribution to that.

He was also particularly attached to one of the elephants: Billie. North spent more than a few hours a week visiting her. Once Jim had roped North into giving Billie a bath—one of the best days of North's life—he was hooked. He'd never been much of an animal person before, but Billie had changed that.

Now all North needed to do was find a life for himself. He wasn't sure how everyone kept coming up with partners. But they did.

Ice walked past just then. She stopped and studied him. "You okay?"

He nodded. "How about you find me a partner too?"

She looked at him in surprise. "Of course. You're next. But I have to admit, most of the time the guys shy away from any active involvement in matchmaking on my part." Her smile widened. "When they choose to go into these kinds of jobs, they seem pretty determined to not fall prey to the magic of love. Like the two don't mix."

He shook his head. "Yeah, but that doesn't mean a whole lot. They end up completely in love by the end of one of their assignments. I'd like to believe in love at first sight, but it's something I've never experienced. Yet, I did see it happening between Liam and Lily."

"Given the relationships that have sprung up around you, there's definitely enough evidence for you to believe in it. But I can't promise anything."

That made him chuckle. "Not expecting any promises."

"Good," she said gently. "Matter of fact, you're heading to England in two days."

He looked at her in surprise. "Why's that?"

"Charles Beckwith, a good friend and supporter in England, has a granddaughter in trouble. Her name is Nikki, and she's en route to his place. He couldn't get the full story out of her but said she was in tears on the phone. It's not minor, but he doesn't know how major it is. He's asked for our delicate touch to help her out."

North frowned. "What kind of trouble?"

"No idea but …" Ice said sadly, "you'll be perfect for the job."

Chapter 1

NORTH GOT OFF the airplane, made his way through customs, and with his one big duffel bag over his shoulder, he stepped outside Heathrow Airport. Within seconds he caught sight of Anders Renau striding toward him. The two men exchanged greetings. Both were newer to Levi's team, but they'd known each other for years.

"How was your flight?" Anders asked.

North shrugged. "Long. But then what do you expect? Texas to London isn't exactly a two-hour hop."

"Hey, just because I was already in Germany doesn't mean it was a piece of cake for me either," Anders joked.

"Ha! It was much easier on you. Besides you were over there visiting friends, weren't you?"

Anders nodded. "More or less. Gathering intel for another job Levi is working on. We're still in the collecting-information stage on that one."

"What do you know about the job we're on now?" North asked.

Anders shook his head. "Not much. Levi called me this morning and said I was booked on the next flight. Something to do with Charles's granddaughter."

"Yes, Nikki Beckwith." North walked behind Anders. "Do you have a ride?"

"Charles sent a car for us."

North followed Anders through the massive airport to the parking lot where the pick ups were. A black sedan with smoked-out windows waited for them, the driver standing outside the vehicle, arms crossed, enjoying the sunshine. But there was no doubt he watched everything going on around him.

"Obviously trained," North said in a low tone.

"Charles has a history. He spends a lot of his time now helping a few of us who are active in the security business."

"What you mean is, he is friends with Levi."

Both men chuckled.

They were quickly in the vehicle and weaving through traffic. The driver never said anything; he just gave them a quick nod, never asking for identification. North thought that was odd until he realized, if their driver was as well trained as North suspected, the guy already had their photo IDs and flights confirmed. He glanced at Anders, who just shrugged.

"Apparently we were expected." He had a big grin on his face, which was pretty typical of Anders. He always had a bright smile and a great sense of humor.

He was a good man, and, if you ever needed somebody to back you up, Anders was always there. North could say that for most of the men who worked for Levi. North knew a lot of them really well, and, even for those he didn't, he still trusted their judgment.

North was delighted to be part of Legendary Security. He'd expected Liam to be traveling with him on this mission, but apparently Liam would be doing something else. That was par for the course with Levi too. Jobs were always coming and going; everybody had something to do. Two more men were available to help out in England, if needed, but, if they weren't, they would head to Holland for something else. It was an exciting lifestyle. And one that, so far, North had found incredibly interesting.

His years as a Navy SEAL had been some of the best years of his life. But, after a couple go-rounds where he saw too much of humanity in its most miserable state and acting impossibly selfish and dangerous, he decided he needed a change. He wasn't so sure Levi could offer North that. It seemed like security work would be so much more of the same military service North had experienced in terms of dealing with the horrors of men plus the incomprehensible bureaucracy at times.

But it wasn't the same in terms of the hierarchy of bosses and the strict rules and regulations. That was something North really appreciated. The brass in the navy were pretty strict. Every layer had new supervisors, new commanders, new top men expecting something else. If you were told to go left, you'd better be already on your way turning left before the order was out of their mouths.

And North understood that at its basic level. It worked for everything that they'd had to do while serving their country in the navy. But, at one point, it became something North wanted to end. He needed something new, something different. So far Levi had been great to work with. North loved the guys he worked with, loved the way Levi's company operated aboveboard, where he could question his orders and offer a better way and have his voice heard and his opinion considered. Although this was only his second mission away, it was interesting work.

"How was Germany?" North asked Anders, more for the sake of small talk than anything.

"Fun. I've had my fill of beer and sausages for a while

though."

North chuckled. "Can anybody really have their fill of that?"

"Yep," Anders said, his grin wide and infectious. "Of course we're in England now, so that means more sausages but boiled this time."

North couldn't stop the shudder inside. "I thought all sausages were supposed to be barbecued," he said half jokingly. He kept his gaze on the traffic, unable to shake off his years of SEAL experience, working on dangerous missions.

He found no sign they were being followed. He'd not noticed anybody keeping track of him at the airport or in the airplane either. So whatever was happening with Charles's granddaughter likely hadn't been extended in his direction. Not that he would have expected it. Levi's crew was relatively unknown over here. And those who were known, MI6 tended to jump on pretty fast. If North or Anders had been on England's watch list, they would have known it once they deplaned.

The vehicle took several corners quickly, one after the other, and North wondered if the driver was shaking off someone tailing them. But then the driver turned into an underground parking lot, pulled up and parked. With a questioning look at Anders, North and Anders confirmed a silent communication between themselves with a simple look. They jumped out, leaving their bags behind and followed the driver.

They ended up at a large elevator going to the sixth floor. "This definitely isn't where Charles lives," North said, his voice low.

Anders nodded. His usual lighthearted laughter was absent. The driver led them to an apartment, where he gave an odd knock sequence, and the door was opened. They stepped inside and waited. Tense, but not terribly worried at this point, North studied everything going on around him.

One man walked forward and said, "What are you two doing here?"

North shoved his hands in his pockets. "Who is asking?"

"My name is Jonas Halpern. I'm MI6, and I'm tired of having way too many Americans coming over and shooting up my city."

North raised his eyebrows. "We're definitely American, but I didn't bring a weapon, and I have no intention of shooting anything," he said coolly. "And I don't know who else you might be talking about."

"So you don't know Badger or Erick?"

North's frown was fast and smooth. "Not by those names, no."

Jonas looked over at Anders and asked, "You?"

"Maybe," Anders said, his voice hard, tight. "What's it to you?"

And that was when it clicked. Badger and Erick, and the rest of their seven-man unit, had been involved in a huge investigation, trying to track down who had betrayed them, causing the major physical and emotional trauma, including loss of limbs, that they'd all experienced in Afghanistan over two years ago.

"Badger was here not all that long ago," Jonas said. "I want to confirm your visit is not related."

"If you talk directly to Levi," Anders said, "then you'll have already received an update on the details in that case."

Jonas glared at him. "I do talk to Levi. More than I care to. This is more of a friendly warning. Mind your *P*s and *Q*s.

No gunfire. No killing any British citizens."

"But other citizens are free game?" North asked with interest. "Because I'm really not sure what nationality we could come up against here."

Jonas's gaze switched to him, and North stared him down.

"We didn't come here to cause trouble," Anders said, his voice deceptively quiet. "And, of course, you're looking after your own country, the same as we would ours. But, if waylaying us from the airport to here is your idea of a friendly visit, I suggest you finish up whatever it is you have to say and allow our driver to take us to our intended destination."

"What makes you think he was forced to come here?"

"I don't think *forced* is the right word," North said. "I'm pretty sure it was more likely *suggested* that he stop here first."

"What are you doing with Charles?"

"Gee, I don't know. Maybe it's a friendly visit." North crossed his arms. "We haven't done anything wrong, so if you've got a problem with us ..."

"I do," Jonas snapped. "Just make sure I don't have a bigger one."

"So then, of course, you'll help with any investigation we end up involved in, correct?"

"No investigations without MI6 involvement." With that Jonas was implacable.

"I tell you what," North offered. "When we find out exactly what the hell is going on, we'll let you know if it involves any British citizens. How's that?"

"When you find out what the hell is going on," Jonas corrected, "you'll tell me exactly what the hell is going on, regardless of who is involved."

"Charles wouldn't tell you?" North asked, sharing a glance with Anders.

"Or Levi? *Interesting*," Anders said with a head tilt to North.

Jonas just glared at the two. He nodded to the driver behind them. Both Americans spun as the door opened, and they walked out.

When they headed toward the elevator, back down to the main floor, into the underground parking, North and Anders discussed this added stop on their visit. North noted, "Interesting guy."

The driver still hadn't said a word.

Anders shook his head. "How very like MI6. Completely cryptic, always watching over everybody, making sure nothing goes wrong. Now if only I was as confident that he was on our side …"

"Oh, I don't think he's on our side at all," North said. "But I do think he's worried about his country."

"We didn't come here to shoot up England or to kill any of its citizens, so he should rest easy with that."

"Ha! If anything, this conversation will make him crazier," North said, perfectly aware that either the elevator was bugged or that the driver was taping the discussion. They got back into the vehicle and waited while the driver exited the parking garage.

When they pulled up in front of a two-story brownstone fifteen minutes later, they got out, not saying a word to the driver, grabbed their bags and walked to the front door before the driver could get there. They hit the door hard with the knocker, and almost instantly Charles opened it. North recognized him from the photos. He'd also seen him on the wall screen at Levi's compound as well.

Charles's face lit up. "North, it's good to meet you in person." He shook North's hand, then gave Anders a big greeting before ushering them inside.

North watched but realized the driver never came in. North filed that away for later. He knew Anders would have also taken note.

"So was that driver yours, or was that MI6's driver?" Anders asked.

Charles sighed. "MI6 is definitely being difficult these days. Sorry about that. I presume you were redirected to talk with Jonas."

"Oh, yeah. Given the standard warning. *Don't shoot any British citizens and no shooting up the city.*"

Charles gave a stiff nod. North imagined, if Charles had been American, he would have given an eye roll. But there was just way too much properness about him for that.

Charles led North and Anders into the sitting room. They dropped their bags in the hallway. Charles said, "I'll take you up to your rooms in a little bit. Come on inside, and let's sit down and have a cup of tea."

North almost choked on the word *tea*. But he was in England. He'd been working on getting a taste for the stuff, but it was a little hard. He was a born-and-bred coffee drinker. Tea seemed like a weak dishwater substitute.

They sat down in the small sitting room and waited until Charles returned with a tray. At least various huge pastries and some kind of a cake were offered on the side. Charles checked his watch, walked over and poured them each a cup. North found it interesting that Charles seemed to be timing the tea.

North accepted the cup with a smile. "Are you ready to

tell us what's going on?"

Charles sighed. "It's circumstantial at best. More like an intuitive guess."

"I've gone with my gut many times." He shared a nod with North.

"It's saved me from even worse disasters. Nothing wrong with an intuitive guess. That's what we start with more times than not," Anders said. "We still need to know what's happening."

"Something to do with your granddaughter," North prompted. "She's in trouble?"

He nodded. "She is, indeed. She doesn't know how much or how bad, and I'm afraid we won't get any warning on the upcoming retaliation. We'll just have trouble on the doorstep in the middle of the night, with the intent to take her out and probably me at the same time. So I've spent the last few nights standing watch while Nikki slept. I would prefer that you not share that with my granddaughter. Now that you two have arrived, we can take shifts for any on-watch duty."

"Of course." North studied the older man's face, seeing the lines of fatigue, the lack of sleep. According to Ice, Charles was normally one of those gentlemen always perfectly dressed, but, right now, as he kept running his fingers through his hair, stray hairs stood out at odd angles. "So tell us how she got into trouble, and what kind of trouble is this?"

"She works for a company in north London. It's an import e-company. She was going over the receiving bills of late and noticed a discrepancy between orders and shipments received. More was received than ordered. Not knowing if she still had a shipment to pay for—or if they'd been overshipped and needed to return the product—she contacted her boss. She couldn't get a hold of him, as he's seriously ill, got his administrative assistant, Hannah, instead. Hannah said Nikki should make a trip to the warehouse to ensure everything was okay because the company didn't have the money to be paying for extra shipments they hadn't ordered. These were cases of wine coming out of France. Supposedly."

"Okay, good place to start. Let me guess. She went to the warehouse and either saw something she wasn't supposed to or, when she was tracking the cases, found out something had been shipped that wasn't supposed to be shipped, and she was seen."

Charles looked at him, and then he slowly nodded his head.

Anders and North both shrugged.

Anders said, "Considering it's imports-exports and shipments, it tends to be drugs or something of value, like stolen artifacts."

"It is, indeed," Charles said with a heavy sigh. He replaced the teacup slowly to the saucer. "She is not sure what she saw though. She opened two of the crates because they were marked as being wine, and, when she got them open, they weren't only wine. The top layer was, but underneath was something else. She didn't have time to inspect these two crates further as she was accosted by two men who asked her what the hell she was doing. Her warehouse guy wasn't there, so she presumed these people worked for the subleasee who shares the same warehouse space.

"When she explained the situation to these two men, they got extremely ugly and said it had nothing to do with her, and she shouldn't stick her nose into something she knew nothing about. The one guy said she should go back to the corporate office and keep her mouth shut."

"But she didn't obviously."

Charles gave him a sharp look and then a hard nod. "You don't really tell Nikki what to do but especially not to keep her mouth shut."

Just then a female's voice erupted from the doorway. "Who are these men, Granddad?"

Charles looked up, a guilty look whispering across his face.

North straightened to greet the new arrival. She was tall, willowy, with red hair down to the middle of her back and a pinched, angry look on her face as she glared at him. He walked a few steps, held out his hand and said, "I'm North Dockter." At her look of surprise, he gave a sad sigh. "I know, right? My parents' idea of a joke." He motioned at Anders. "This is my friend Anders Renau."

She gave her head a shake, reached out and shook his hand. "I'm sorry for you. That must have been pretty rough in school."

He nodded. "It was. But only for the first little while," he said curtly. "I learned to fight off the bullies pretty darn fast."

"Good, then you won't have a problem with my temper," she snapped. She turned and glared at Charles. "Granddad, why are they here?"

Charles straightened. "Levi sent them over to help. Two other men are close by and will come if we need them."

"Why is it everybody goes to Levi for assistance?" she asked suspiciously.

"Because he's a great help," North said. "And, no, we aren't taking advantage of your grandfather."

She sniffed. "I think somebody else needs to be the judge

of that."

But Charles shook his head. "That is not under discussion, Nikki."

She gave him a flat look. "And neither is my business."

"I think it's a little late for that," Anders said gently. "The minute you start dealing with irregular shipments into the UK, you're talking about having a major problem."

"Can you describe the man who warned you away?" North asked.

She gave a clipped nod. "His name tag read Carl. I think the second man's name tag was Phillip."

North considered the names and then said, "Interesting. Do you think they were the right men to wear those designated shirts? Or were they wearing somebody else's uniform? Not that it matters at this stage. More important is, why were they hassling you? You had as much right to be there as they did. Even more that they shouldn't have known or cared about your company's business."

She shrugged. "I have no idea why they were upset about my visit to the warehouse."

"Who have you told?"

"About what?"

North just stared at her.

She jutted out her jaw. "Okay, fine. I told my boss's assistant, Hannah, and I told Granddad."

"What did the assistant say?"

"She said she didn't know anything about it. She figured it was just a clerical error."

"And she had no solution as to how to fix it?"

"I don't think she particularly cared to fix it," Nikki said drily. "Our boss is dying, and she's his close friend. The business is for sale, but I don't believe there's been much interest."

"And how long have you been bringing this particular wine product into the country?"

"I don't know," she said. "It never occurred to me to look at that." She stared, her gaze going from one man to the other. "Why? What do you think is happening?"

"Smuggling of course," North said. "But whether it's drugs or stolen goods, it's hard to determine. If it's drugs, then, of course, we want to know how long this product has been moved because it would give us an idea of how big the supply chain is."

She paled, her lips pinched together. "I don't like the way you think."

"Well, the way I think tends to keep people alive," North said. "In your case, you've already been threatened once. How long do you want to keep working that whole denial thing before you realize this is bigger than what you were expecting it to be?"

"I'm not sure I'm in denial. I just didn't know what to do. I figured I overreacted when Carl threatened me, and I called Granddad. He's dealt with a lot of this in his life, and I figured he would know what to do this time too."

"Of course. I called Levi. I also called Bullard."

"I'd like to go to Bullard's just once," North said appreciatively. "I've heard a lot about his new compound."

"I don't think it's quite ready yet," Charles said. "They stayed here recently when work was being done. And, of course, Kasha goes back and forth with Brandon all the time."

"Those are the people you've not wanted me to meet," Nikki said impatiently. "You never share much about your constant visitors."

"I'm sure Charles appreciates them stopping by," Anders said. "That's part of your grandfather's business."

"So I'm supposed to share about my business, and he doesn't have to share about his?"

"That pretty much sums it up," North said cheerfully. "Besides, you haven't given us a whole lot of information. So, if the crates only had one top layer of wine, with whatever else underneath, did too many cases come in or not enough cases?"

"Too many. I confirmed the tally on the wine because, at that kind of cost, my company doesn't have the money to cover what ended up being thirty spare cases."

"That would be a decent price tag, depending on which wine it was. But, if you do this on a regular basis, is that not something you can distribute to whoever your boss wholesales to? And who is that?"

At that question, she barked, "That's confidential. I can't really tell you who it is we brought it in for."

"You'll have to," North said in exasperation. "Do you realize maybe that extra shipment was requested as well?"

"I already contacted them and confirmed their order, and it's the same order I had on my paperwork. They ordered thirty cases, not sixty."

"Sure, but have you checked the other orders for thirty cases to see if that was really wine being delivered or if it was simply a layer of camouflage for something else as well?"

Her gaze widened, and he could see she hadn't considered this.

"Smugglers already have a system in place," he said gently. "It could be that it was just a numbers mistake. But that doesn't mean the original thirty shipped to you were the product you expected either."

"And how does customs handle all these?" Anders asked.

"Everything is cleared on the shipping docks. We've never had a problem," she said, "so I'm not sure what this is all about."

"If they hadn't threatened you, you wouldn't have thought anything of it, would you?"

"No," she admitted.

"But with Carl's and Phillip's extra attention on you and these particular cases, you would have investigated further, correct?"

"Of course." She hesitated, looking at her grandfather for added reassurance.

"You can trust these men as much as you trust me, Nikki. They are here to protect you from whatever ugliness you have unwittingly discovered." When she remained undecided, Charles added, "And they will protect me too, while you remain here in my home until this is all resolved. It is not safe for you to return to your apartment alone."

With a soft nod and a grim set to her mouth, she finally opened up to the two strangers in her grandfather's home. "I did wonder what else was in the case. If I could have confirmed that, I would have contacted the company, asked about the secondary contents, requested a corrected manifest and proper documentation. Then, if I was satisfied with the paperwork, I'd have asked if they were looking for any more cases, as we'd accidentally been shipped an excess amount.

"If they didn't want the duplicated order, I'd look at other suppliers, see if they wanted them. If not, it would go back to the wholesaler," she admitted. "When the men accosted me in the warehouse, I was escorted out. I started to head home to my apartment but got nervous, since I do live alone and don't really know my neighbors at all. I called

Granddad then, came here and called in sick the next day at work."

"How far away is the business from the apartment where you live?"

"It's about a half-hour drive in to work, depending on the traffic," she said.

"And did you bring copies of the manifest? And the purchase orders?"

She frowned, her fingers clenching around her hip bones as if considering how to answer that question.

"We can't help you if we don't know all the details."

"I don't want to bring trouble down on the company that they can't afford to handle."

"What other stuff does this company import?"

"All kinds of specialty goods. Food, wine products, dry goods."

"And how long has the business been open?"

"Over one hundred years," she said. "My boss inherited the company from his father, who inherited it from his father."

"And does your boss have a son who he will pass on the business to?"

"No. As I said, he was looking to sell it. He has no children and no close family. He's planning to give the proceeds from the sale to charities."

North filed away that information. "Interesting future."

"Why? Don't you believe a man has the right to do what he wants with his own assets?"

"Absolutely. The question is, who doesn't want him to do that with his assets because they think they have a better use for them?"

"No one," she said quietly. "Only a handful of us work

for the company. There is no one else."

NIKKI STUDIED THE men in front of her. She knew some of what her grandfather did but not the full extent of it. There was something military, unyielding, about these two men. As if there was nothing in life they couldn't handle. She could really use some of that particular brand of confidence herself.

The men in the warehouse had terrified her. Something about their features, the tones of their voices, everything about them said that, if she said the wrong word sideways, they'd have broken her neck and tossed her into the river. She'd panicked; no doubt about it now. She currently felt foolish thinking she had made too much out of nothing back then. But she didn't know quite what to do about it.

She didn't even know how Granddad could possibly know men like this, like the pair in his home. But thinking about it further, she'd seen others of this same cut of cloth come through as well. But Granddad has done his best to separate her from them instantly. More often than not, she just knew they were coming through but hadn't actually seen them.

Once her parents had moved to Switzerland, she'd spent more time with her grandfather. At the time she had thought it would be nice to keep the old man company but then realized he was far from lonely and far from an old man.

They had had an interesting relationship. There was a lot of affection on both sides, and she certainly wouldn't want anything to happen to him. Not only that, when she had found herself in trouble, he'd been the first one she had called. Her parents still didn't know.

She had a brother, but he was in med school in the US.

He was also the opposite of these men in front of her. He lived for science, lived for every kind of surgical procedure. He would be a general surgeon at first but told her eventually he would focus on specialties of the brain. She couldn't think of anything she wanted to know less about. The thought of someone cutting into her brain made her cringe. She couldn't even watch those fake brain surgeries on TV as part of a police series, much less the real surgeries filmed for a documentary. The sight of the blood and exposed brain matter gave her the chills.

She was happy to be managing imports and exports. She didn't have a problem dealing with all the related paperwork, although she would certainly get frustrated when the government stepped in and made her fill out yet more documents for various things. But she'd been doing this for the last five years, and she had become comfortable with it. Until this. And these men before her were right; she hadn't pulled the records to see how much of this particular wine the company had ordered on a regular basis. All she'd done was ask how many cases were supposed to be in this order. The answer had been instantaneous. *As always, thirty cases.*

She hadn't even checked to see how often they ordered. In fact, she'd just run.

Abruptly she raised one finger, turned and walked away from the sitting room. She ran lightly up the stairs to her bedroom, grabbed her laptop and returned. The men had seated themselves again, sipping tea, eating the sweets Granddad always ended up baking. She didn't know if he loved baking or if he just loved feeding the mysterious strangers who came through his place. She sat down in a single upright chair and turned on her laptop. "I'm checking to see if I can access the records from here."

"Do you work from home normally?"

"Yes," she said.

"What about logging in from this location though?"

She looked up with a frown. "Am I putting my grandfather in danger?"

North shook his head. "Not any more than you already have," he said gently. "We just want to double-check that, with the new IP address, it wouldn't be unusual for you to be here."

"No, it's not unusual," she said slowly. "I have been here before. And sometimes I've had work to do here as well. Granddad was sick a couple months back, and I stayed here for several days."

North looked over at Charles. "Are you doing okay now?"

Charles nodded. "When she says *sick*, what she means is, I broke my arm up high near the shoulder. I was doing fine, but she wanted to babysit."

She gave him a warm smile. "Maybe I wanted a few days to spend time with you."

Charles's face softened. "Ditto. But you can come and spend time with me without me having to break something. You know that, right?"

She chuckled. "Good thing," she said, "because I don't really want to have to break something myself to have you return the favor." She logged into her work's database. "I'm logged in now. And I'm bringing up the distributor that ordered the wine."

"What company is it?"

"Only the Best," she said. "They have several outlets they distribute to. We bring their products into the country, then make deliveries to their own specialty stores."

"Are they an end user?"

She looked up, frowning at him. "If you mean, are they selling the wine at a restaurant to people, no. I don't believe so. I think they sell it to the restaurant, which then turns around and sells it to the patrons of the restaurants."

"And wholesalers?"

She shrugged. "I don't know too much about their business, but I would presume so."

"Interesting." North tucked away that information. "How much do they normally order?"

"I'm going through their order history right now. ... Looks to be thirty cases of this product every three months."

"And you have no way to know if that's a lot or a little or involved any kind of a change as to the individual wine or amount or frequency of delivery over time?"

"I don't know if it's a lot or a little, but it hasn't changed for two years," she said, flicking through the screenloads of pages. "They started with us two years ago. Thirty cases every three months." She looked up, over the top of the laptop. "Do you need to know anything else?"

"Yes," Anders said. "What else do they order through you?"

She searched the database by the company name and came up with two other products. "They ordered champagne and oils," she said with a frown. "Gourmet olive oils."

"By the cases?"

She nodded. "Yes, twenty cases per month."

"Isn't that a lot of olive oil?"

She shook her head. "Not really. Depending on what they're using it for and who they're selling it to. We have companies that bring in hundreds of cases in a month."

"So are these suppliers of these orders on the up-and-up,

and you've dealt with them a lot over the last five years you've been with the company?"

"That's a different search," she muttered, typing away into the database. She brought up the supplier of the thirty cases of wine. "Yes, but this is not the maker of the wine. They bring it in from Italy and Spain apparently. It goes to France—where they sell it to us. We buy it, turn around and sell it to the company here."

"So typical distribution channels."

She shrugged. "Some. There is a tendency to go as direct as you can with winemakers. But often they have contracts, so we get it from whoever holds the contracts."

"Any sign of any irregularities in all these years?"

She lifted her gaze again. "No, not that I know of. But I haven't looked, and I've never come across anything like this."

"So what really alerted you was the fact that you had a double shipment?"

"Yes, like I said. The question was whether my company had ordered twice the amount, but, as I told you, they didn't. So I went to the warehouse to ensure we were talking about the same product. And there the men came at me and told me to get the hell out."

"Is it your warehouse? So the export company owns the property?" Anders asked. "Or do you lease space in a big warehouse from someone else?"

She glanced up in a surprise. "That's exactly what we do. We lease out the entire space. But it's a massive warehouse. It is our only warehouse, but we lease space out to someone else."

"And who is that?"

"Booker & Sons," she said. "And we've done this for

years now. We had the original lease on the building, but we didn't need all the space, and income is income, so we lease out part of it. It's well set up in the warehouse district with lots of loading bays, easy access. It's just space. Booker has been using it for a long time now."

"Then we need to double-check that Booker hasn't further subleased part of that space to yet another company. If they didn't need their space, that's an easy way to bring in money for them too."

She frowned. "I don't think so. They asked for more space for themselves a year ago. Besides, they're not allowed to sublease any of the space they lease from us. It's in their contract."

Charles chuckled. "Just because people aren't allowed to do something doesn't stop them from doing it. Particularly if they're in financial difficulties, they'll do their own sublease without you knowing about it."

She sniffed. "That would be highly irregular and would not make my boss very happy at all. He's always been very exclusive as to who uses his space. But, I have to admit, he's not very involved in the business anymore."

"How old is he?"

"He's only sixty-six, I believe," she said slowly. "But he's got cancer, and the treatments aren't working."

"Hence him wanting to sell," Anders said. "There's nothing quite like an unpleasant diagnosis to make you reevaluate your life and your end-of-life decisions."

"He made it well known to his employees that he had the company up for sale. How it might not survive in its current business format. So that we could make contingency plans. I've been squirrelling away a little more money from each paycheck, just in case the end comes sooner than later," she admitted.

"And, if you've been with this import-export company for five years," North added, "you know the ins and outs. It's quite likely that whoever buys the company might want your continued assistance, even after the transfer."

"Maybe," she said steadily. "I have to admit that had been my first thought. But often they hire you for a little while, and then you're very quickly relieved of your position as they hire their own staff."

"And you can't really blame them for that either," Anders said. "When you think about it, that's just good business practice."

She winced. "Maybe. I'll be looking for a job regardless."

"Can you send me any other company details you may have to my email?" North asked. He pulled out his phone and gave her his email address. "I want to do some research into the history of every company we've just discussed, from Booker & Sons, to the company that's importing the wine, Only the Best, and also the supplier of the wine. And I want the address of that warehouse as well."

She brought up an email and typed in the requested names and addresses. When she was done, she checked it over and hit Send. "Okay, that's the information I have."

"Great. Now, how good is your memory of what this guy looks like who threatened you?"

"Men," she corrected quietly. "There were two of them. Swarthy, as if they were maybe Corsican, Sicilian, dark Italians, a nationality like that, although I'm not very good at distinguishing ethnicities. Their English was extremely good. Their diction was clear, while they did have an accent, but again I couldn't tell you what for sure."

"Good. Ages?"

She shrugged. "Mid-forties?"

After that came more questions until finally she said, "Honestly I don't have anything else to tell you."

"We do need the admin's name and contact information, plus the boss's name and contact information." This came from Anders.

North looked at him, then glanced at Nikki to see what reaction they would get. And, as he suspected, she was already shaking her head.

"No, I can't have you contacting them."

"I don't want to contact them. I want to start searching their phone numbers and addresses and emails," Anders said. "We have to rule out if anyone in the company is involved in this."

Her jaw dropped as she stared at him. "They definitely aren't involved. What the hell made you go in that direction?"

Silence ascended in the small room.

"And you can't just hack into these people's lives." She shifted her gaze from one to the other and finally to her granddad. "Granddad, what is it that I don't know?"

Chapter 2

N IKKI STUDIED HER grandfather, seeing the intelligence gleaming in the back of his eyes. "Does this have something to do with what you secretly do all the time?"

He gave her a bland look.

She raised both hands in frustration. "Somebody start talking."

"Your grandfather has been of great assistance to a lot of people," North said firmly. "Like us, he can't give too many details. But that doesn't mean he doesn't know a lot and hasn't been involved in a lot. But it's all on the up-and-up, and it's all related to security on an international level. And, in that line of work, there has always been a certain amount of intelligence gathering, whether about smuggling or terrorists or trafficking of people," he said.

"So do you have any connections who can track this down, Granddad?"

He nodded. "That's also why I brought in Levi and his crew. Once it starts getting life-and-death dangerous, we can't do everything ourselves, my dear."

"I didn't get a chance to look too closely at what was under the wine."

"Exactly. So what we need to do is go to your ware-house, find the crates and check it out ourselves," North said.

"Which brings up the question," Anders added, "how does the merchandise travel from the warehouse to its final destination?"

"We use several transport companies. Stan, our warehouse guy, handles all this," she said. "You're not breaking into the warehouse, are you?"

North looked up in surprise. "Didn't you just say it was your warehouse?"

Feeling foolish, she nodded slowly. "Yes, I suppose that's true. Except for the Booker & Sons section."

"Do you have anything in your contract that says you can't go into your own warehouse, even the sublet section?"

She shook her head. "No, of course not. That's why I went down there to check out the misdelivery myself."

"Right. So, if we enter the warehouse and check out its contents, surely that won't cross anybody?"

She sighed, snapped her laptop closed, hugged it up against her chest and said, "It's just that all this feels wrong. I'm questioning everything right now."

"Good," he said. "You should. Until we get to the bottom of this, we trust no one, and we look at everything three times, and then we check it a fourth time if there's any inkling inside us that something is wrong."

Her gaze drifted to her granddad. "Are you okay with that plan?"

Charles leaned forward, reached out and grasped her hand in his. "Absolutely. This is how we do business from now on. These guys will come up with a plan. I'll okay it, and you will let us go ahead with it."

She wrinkled her face at that. "You know I don't like taking orders."

"No, you never have," he said with a gentle smile. "And

these aren't orders, but neither are they suggestions. Once you put something like this into motion, we need to let it happen. If you're worried at all, then let's get to the bottom of this."

She opened her mouth and said, "Honestly I was starting to think it was just my imagination."

Her grandfather shook his head. "You might think it was your imagination, but I saw you and heard you right afterward. You know exactly who you called and why."

She gave him a smile. "So true. There didn't seem to be anybody else I could call, so I guess *thank you* is in order." She looked at the two men. "The thing is, I can't pay you. And I cannot authorize the company to pay you either."

North looked at her in amusement.

She frowned at him. "This isn't funny."

"No, it isn't. Pride is a very useful thing to have and to work with. And that's fine that you can't pay us because we already got paid."

She thrummed her fingers on her laptop and looked at her granddad. "Are you paying them?"

He shook his head. "Levi is doing this as a favor for me."

She stared at him suspiciously. "A favor for what?"

He patted her hand again. "Nothing for you to worry about. I've helped out Levi lots of times. When I needed somebody to call, it was him I called. He's happy to help me."

Realizing she sounded more churlish than she meant to, her shoulders sagged, and she faced the two newcomers. "Then the least I can do is take you upstairs to show you to your rooms, and then we'll get you some dinner." She bounced to her feet and waited for the two men to stand. She glanced at the teapot, their teacups still full and grinned.

"When you come down, I'll put on some coffee." The relief on North's face made her laugh out loud. "You're so American."

"You're so British," he said.

"Actually I spent more years in California than I care to remember."

"Why were you there?"

"I went to UCLA for my degree."

"Yet you decided not to stay?"

"I did for several years, and then I thought about coming home again. I had a hankering to get back to English soil, and I started working over here. It's been great, but it's coming to an end. Now I have no clue what I'll do."

"You're pretty sure the company will be sold quickly?"

"Or shut down. I don't see how the boss can keep going. I can't even get ahold of him to ask him questions anymore. It's always his assistant now."

"Do you share an office?"

"With his cancer diagnosis, he set up an office in his house because he can't do the traveling anymore. So I now work from home mostly. It saves money for the company. We do have two other staff members who work out of a much smaller corporate office. I could have joined them there, and I do go there once a week or so, if needed. But, other than that, I work remotely. I handle the import and export paperwork, and the men in the office take the orders and handle sales."

"That must be nice," North said.

She shot him a look. "It would be, but it also reminds you how your job is coming to an end. At least in an office setting, you meet people, have a business network. You have a social life and a feel for how things are going. But, when you're removed from that, going in once a week makes you feel more like a guest, a visitor, an outsider, and you see the changes that are happening faster. So, every time I go in, it seems like everybody is less and less busy, people are quieter, less jovial. I believe this has been happening for the last few months now, and I think we're probably coming to the end. I don't know what will happen if the owner dies before he sells the company."

"Well, it's also possible somebody realizes the business is in trouble and has taken advantage of your distribution system to do a bit more smuggling than is expected."

"*Expected?* None is expected."

"Unfortunately a lot more smuggling is going on than any of us want to consider," North said. "The smugglers are just getting more sophisticated."

"That's quite possible but never with our company," she said firmly. She led the way up the stairs, and, at the top, she pointed to two rooms opposite each other. "One on each side." She walked to the one on the right, opened the door and motioned at North. "This one is yours. In a straight line down there is a rooftop exit and fire escapes down either side."

"Interesting that you would tell me that."

She snorted. "You look like the kind of guy who will immediately find the first way out now that you've arrived."

She spoke in such a dry tone that he had to laugh. "True enough."

She motioned to the door on the opposite side. "Anders, this room is for you." She opened it to show a duplicate room. But the color scheme was very different.

"These are nice rooms," Anders said, stepping in. "Nice suites, big beds."

She nodded and smiled. "Very true. Granddad has been here for decades. It was his parents' house before him."

"And maybe, if you're lucky, it'll be yours one day." North looked at her and added, "Do you have other family?"

"A brother in the States and my parents, who live in Switzerland."

He nodded. "At least you have Charles right now."

She gave North a sad smile. "Yes, but seeing my boss waste away just reminds me that my grandfather is that much older than my boss. Although I have him right now, how much longer will he be around?"

North gently squeezed her shoulder. "The thing is, you do have him now. There's no guarantee of tomorrow for any of us. So enjoy what you've got while you've got it, and, if fate steps in and takes him from you, then be grateful for the days you took the time to enjoy him. And he has to look at the same thing from his point of view. There's no guarantee for any of us. We're here today, but we all can be gone tomorrow."

NORTH QUICKLY UNLOADED his bag, grabbed his laptop and stepped out of his room. He waited at the top of the stairs for Anders to do the same, and the two marched downstairs with their laptops and cell phones. They returned to the same sitting room they'd been in before. It was empty at the moment, but that was fine. They had some research to do. They needed to check in with Levi also.

North emailed Levi to say they had arrived safely, met Jonas and then gave Levi the story about Nikki, as much as he knew at the moment. After he hit Send, he opened up a new Google page and started researching the import-export company that Nikki worked for. Then North forwarded Nikki's email list of related names, companies and addresses to Levi.

When they went on a job like this, North had to keep reminding himself how he was no longer in the military, with its covert ops and segmented partitions to add further levels of secrecy, akin to the right hand not knowing what the left hand did. Plus, it was an added disconnect between what the SEALs did and the resulting effects. In many ways all the secrecy probably hindered a lot of cases of PTSD among the troops, since they didn't have a clear picture of what went down. Not the actual details.

But working for Levi was a job with layers and layers of transparency, even among Levi and Ice and all the other guys. The guys never went anywhere alone while on assignment; they were always in constant communication with the control room team at the compound. Research was done in conjunction with everyone else. Sometimes the men in the field didn't get a chance to do very much research at all. They relied on people back at their base of operations to fill in the holes.

As soon as he sent off that list, North looked at Anders. "I don't know about you, but I want to head to that warehouse first."

"Exactly." Anders looked at his wristwatch and frowned. "It's not open now."

"Even better," he said. "She works for the company, so she should have keys or digital access to the building."

"We don't exactly have permission from the owner though," Anders said. "Just from her. Although the admin did give her permission to go and check it out initially."

North considered the matter, then gave a clipped nod.

"That should do it. We have permission from the head office and from her. But I don't want her to come with us."

"Too damn bad," came Nikki's hard voice.

With a big grin North looked up to catch Nikki's gaze as she snapped at Anders. "I understand why North is saying that," she said.

Anders nodded, adding, "A—we can move quieter if it's just the two of us. And B—we don't want to put you in danger."

"According to you two," she said in a slightly more mollified tone of voice, "I'm already in danger. Besides, you'll need me to show you which part of the warehouse is ours versus the other company's."

"Are you telling me that you can't draw a map for us?" North asked.

She thought about it and shook her head. "I'm not sure I could. I was quite confused when I was there myself."

"In which case," Anders said smoothly, "you won't be any help now."

The tray of coffee mugs she carried landed with a hard *bang* on the coffee table. She straightened, crossed her arms over her chest and tapped her foot on the floor. "I get that you're here in some sort of weird hero mentality, but it's not working for me. So I highly suggest you get off that macho horse of yours and realize that I'm going with you, whether you like it or not." She spun around on her heels and left.

North burst out laughing.

Anders glared at his buddy. "You *would* like her," he muttered. "She's just your type."

North leaned forward. "I have a type?"

Anders nodded. "You like them *spitfirey* and difficult to get along with."

"How could you possibly know that?" North asked in confusion. "I don't think you've even met any of the women I went out with."

"No, but I already know you like Nikki, which means she's your type. And, for that, you need to have your head examined," he said.

North shot him a look. "I didn't say I liked her."

"Well, the two of you respond to each other very well," he said drily. "A little too well. So I hope you don't start doing any of that lovebird gushy stuff around me."

"Why? You don't like that stuff?"

"Not when I'm not the one doing it." Anders chuckled. "And I have no intention of playing third wheel to anybody."

"I never really understood that saying," North said. "I mean, surely if you've got two wheels, being a third wheel would be more stable. Like a tricycle."

Anders glared at him, snagged a large mug of coffee and set it down on the coffee table beside him. "For that comment, you get the smaller cup."

"Hey, that's not fair." North grabbed the remaining cup for himself. "She meant the big cup for me," he murmured.

"Good. In that case, I'm glad I stole it. And I'm not so sure about this London Emporium company she works for. Doesn't that word *emporium* generally mean *anything and everything*?"

"We need a better understanding of the products they're importing and exporting," North said. "And will need deep background checks on everyone who works for them too."

"According to their website they outsource anything. Of course that's a blanket statement. But they do talk about rare wines, imported cheeses, specialty gourmet foods, like …

octopus … noodles." The words slowly dripped off his tongue, and his face twisted at the thought. "Why would anybody want to eat that?"

"I think it's black octopus too," North said, thinking about it. "I believe they're handmade in a small town in Italy or some such thing."

Anders just shook his head and kept on reading. "So they do all kinds of specialty food items, including wines and spirits. But they also do dry goods. So high-end linens out of a special area in France, unique wool from Aran Islands, Ireland. But don't these places already import and export?"

"They do. There are always middlemen with connections to make the flow of goods easier."

"Plus hand-blown crystal out of Italy, wine glasses from Venice—which is Italy anyway, so I don't know why that's listed separately," he muttered.

"Because, with anything out of Venice, you get to tack on some more money," North said with a chuckle. "But this is interesting. They also bring in gold and silver."

"Jewelry?" Anders asked.

"We should be asking her all these questions," North said. "She'll have a better idea about all the products they import."

"I do know what we import," she said from the doorway. "But we'll discuss it after we eat. Come now, please. Dinner is ready."

The two men closed their laptops, placed them off to the side and stood, following her into the kitchen.

North was amazed as Nikki led them into a formal dining room set for four. He stared at the length of the table and said, "You could easily feed a dozen people here."

"My grandfather does regularly," she murmured as she

took a seat. She pointed at the chair beside her own. "Sit please."

He did. "Are you sure there's nothing I can do to help?"

She smiled and shook her head.

From across the table Anders muttered, "Suck-up."

North snorted. "Being nice doesn't mean I'm trying to be a flirt. Or to get into her good graces."

"Well, one of us should," Anders said with a big grin focused on Nikki. "Apparently she doesn't like me."

Nikki snorted but stayed quiet.

North smiled. Anders was a good man with a big heart and smile. And, when he made a good first impression, he tended to settle into that mode and didn't give a damn what anybody else thought. That was all fine and dandy, until somebody he liked couldn't see him for who he really was. North grinned at the disgruntled look on his friend's face.

"So you both used to be SEALs? Why did you leave the US Navy?" Nikki asked, joining in the conversation now.

"The navy way was getting to be too much," Anders said. "The missions, the fighting, just the constant immersion into the depths of human depravity. My spirit sank every time I was called to go anywhere. I was fighting it mentally, and, once that set in, it was time to leave."

"Agreed," North said. "I felt like there was so much more need for all of us elsewhere, and yet we were doing so very little to help in the broadest sense while in the service. That was frustrating. I wanted to do more every place we went, but we were always under strict orders to not do anything other than what we were expressly told to do. The orders were starting to chafe."

"They had chafed on me for a long time," Anders continued. "At least with Levi, you understand why the orders are there. While we were on SEALs missions, outside of those orders to ensure our survival by our own team leaders and commanders in the field with us, the rest of those corporate-issued orders often made no sense, probably coming from some guy in a suit in his posh Washington, DC, office, who probably never served his country on a battlefield. We couldn't discuss them, get them changed or ask for somebody to reconsider them. In Levi's case, he's always willing to listen."

Nikki quietly watched their animated expressions as the guys spoke, seemingly taking in every word.

North nodded. "I think it's great we're both working for Levi now. Not to mention Stone and Merk and Rhodes are all in the next tier, and, because we're all of the same mindset and background, we all understand how much the naval orders used to cause us trouble. There was nothing more inane than stupid orders that led men to their deaths."

"Ditto that."

They heard a faint rumbling sound, and, as they watched, Charles pushed a trolley toward the table. It was heavily laden with food.

North sniffed the air appreciably. "Well, there's definitely an advantage to being here with you, Charles. This food smells divine."

"Have you been around Alfred's cooking much?" Nikki asked as she waited for her grandfather to lift off the lids from the platters.

"Not enough yet," North said. "And Bailey's baking is unbelievable. It's not a hardship to wake up to fresh croissants and cinnamon buns every morning."

The heady aroma of fresh roast beef filled the air. North smiled and held out his plate in anticipation. There was gravy, mashed potatoes and roasted vegtables. He was in heaven.

Charles chuckled as he proceeded to fill North's plate to overflowing. "Exactly. Levi's outfit has gotten so big that Alfred needed a competent hand in the kitchen. Sounds like he's found quite a gem in Bailey."

The other plates were filled, Nikki's was only half as full as his. North worried that she wasn't eating enough. But she appeared to be delighted with the fare in front of her. North, satisfied, continued with the conversation. "And honestly I think she's quite happy there. They are two peas in a pod. They never get more excited than when you bring home a new cookbook or suggest we try Tunisian food for a change. They start tossing ideas back and forth, and we know it'll be a fabulous dinner," North said with a chuckle. "I swear to God that's half the reason why Levi can keep us, due to Alfred's and Bailey's cooking."

"And I hear you have puppies."

"Well, they are definitely big now. I don't know about calling them puppies anymore," North said. "I couldn't believe it when I first arrived and saw the dogs running wild inside and outside of the main structure. But it makes sense. The compound includes a lot of acreage, and there are a lot of people to look after the dogs. Alfred and Bailey took one, and he has become the kitchen mascot. He's called Orange."

Nikki looked up. "*Orange?*"

North shot her a grin even as he cut the melt-in-your-mouth beef. "Yes. You have to keep oranges away from him. He thinks they're balls, and he's forever biting down on them and then yelping when the orange juice gets in his mouth. But he won't give them up because he swears they're balls, and those balls are his."

At that Nikki chuckled. "And I suppose they keep the oranges in a bowl on the counter instead of in the fridge."

"Absolutely. And the puppy, Orange, is well known for hopping up onto a chair, snagging an orange out of the bowl and running off with it."

Anders admitted, "It's quite adorable."

At that, Charles's smile lightened the atmosphere, and the rest of the conversation while they ate was about Levi's business and how he was adding to the compound.

"They broke ground on the swimming pool," North said. "I know we're all waiting for that. It was delayed multiple times, but it's going ahead now."

Charles nodded. "I'm glad. That's Ice's project. She loves to swim."

"I do too," Nikki said. "But I don't ever expect to have my own pool in England. Of course the weather is better in Texas for swimming."

"That's the advantage of a pool at Levi's place. A lot of people live there, either in the compound itself or within the individual apartments that are being continuously built to meet the demand. So that pool will get a lot of use. So will the massive outdoor kitchen going in and the large patio space."

"It's nice to know Levi's dream has come true," Charles noted.

"Still, it's a big complex, high-security type place?" Nikki asked.

Anders nodded. "Absolutely. That's one of the beauties of it. Everybody lives inside the secured perimeter walls, but it's very much a home at the compound. More of an industrial-type mansion with so many of us living there. Not like Bullard's main location, which is more ornate in its exterior design. But Levi and Ice have rehabbed a lot of apartments in one of the other buildings, so a lot of the couples have their own places that are a bit set apart from the rest of us. They often don't eat in Alfred's kitchen, but there are always leftovers so that nobody ever runs short of food. And I don't think Alfred is ever happier than when he has the whole gang around. Often they host Sunday barbecues, and, now that the new outdoor kitchen is getting set up, I'm sure that'll be more than a one-day-a-week thing."

"There's nothing like a barbecue," Charles said with a big smile. "I have a small pit out on the back patio, but it's definitely not intended to feed more than a couple people."

"Exactly. I think that's why Alfred is in his heaven over there. There aren't too many complexes like it."

"Except for Bullard's place. Alfred said he has something very similar, although Bullard's is grander in its architecture," Charles noted.

"As far as I understand," Anders said, "Bullard's got his newest complex close to the Tunisia border, in addition to his original African estate."

North's plate was rapidly emptying. He eyed the platters wondering if seconds would be offered. He did enjoy home-cooked food.

Charles nodded. "Yes, and it's calming down a bit now. He's finally got enough staff to run both places. I think he still prefers his original estate as his main station. After all, he did all the landscaping himself."

"Do you keep in touch with him?" North wondered how that worked. Charles was kind of a middleman for everybody, and yet he appeared to know Alfred and maybe Dave very well.

"Alfred, Dave and I are old friends, although I'm older

than the other two," Charles said with a smile as he stood up and refilled North's plate. "We've all served in the same military, were all in similar jobs and met through Levi and Bullard. The fourth one of us, Byron, has gone on to handle the kitchens at the new complex for Bullard."

"Wow," North said in respect, his gaze lifting to study Charles's face. "That's wonderful to hear. And a nice way for the four of you to keep in touch."

"I don't keep in touch as much as the others do. They have some sort of security system with monitors where they can keep track of each other on a regular basis."

"I've seen that, but I think the TV system they have works a little better now. Although the TV is a special monitor, they can beam in live from Bullard's complex. You don't have that here, do you?" North asked, looking around.

Charles shook his head. "No, I don't have a working base with a computer linkup like they each do. I'm more of a middleman. It's just me and my property. I'm always opening my door to help out when I can," he said quietly. "But I'm not sure I'm interested in doing a whole lot more than that. I'm not as young as I used to be."

North glanced at Nikki and realized she had to be at least thirty herself and, if not, then close to it.

She patted her granddad's hand. "You're doing just fine. You already do an awful lot more than most people do," she admitted. "It keeps your hand in the game, which I know is important to you."

Charles chuckled. "It does, indeed. We've had quite the events at this place. Trouble comes in all forms and from many different directions, including yours, my dear."

She wrinkled her face. "I was hoping it wouldn't be me with security troubles. It would have been nice not to add to your burdens."

"It's not a burden," he said. "You're family. And I'll do anything in my power to help you."

North watched the exchange, seeing the obvious affection and caring between the two of them. "At least you know who to call on when you need any additional help. Speaking of which, we want to go to the warehouse tonight."

Startled, she looked at him in surprise. "Why tonight?"

Anders and North exchanged glances. North shrugged, spoke to Anders. "We could use her help."

"We could, but she could also get us killed. *That* we don't need."

"I promise I'll do whatever you tell me to do when you tell me to do it," Nikki interjected.

Even North raised an eyebrow at her. "Somehow I don't think I can believe that," he said gently. "You care too much. Your own grandfather said you don't like taking orders. However, I understand that you want to get to the bottom of this, and you want to find the men who threatened you. So, if we say, *Go left*, and you see them go right, you'll go right."

She sat back with a huff gently nudging her empty plate to the side. Then shrugged. "You still need me." She glanced at her watch. "It's heading on nine o'clock. We're about thirty-five minutes away. We could be back by midnight."

"Do you have the weekend off?" North asked, considering the amount she'd eaten, then realized she'd cleaned her plate and was even now snagging up a fresh bun and buttering it. She'd be fine tonight.

She nodded. "I work from home anyway, remember?"

They helped Charles clean off the table and do the dishes. But the kitchen was small and crowded with them all in it. North watched as Nikki shifted impatiently, running rapid-fire through the kitchen, speeding up the process. Finally Charles shooed them all away. "Go. I'll get this done much faster without all this 'assistance.'"

"Meet me out front in five minutes," Nikki said, looking from North to Anders, getting an acknowledging nod from both. Then she promptly left.

North leaned over, squeezed Charles's shoulder and said, "Thanks. And, yes, we'll look after her."

Charles gripped his fingers with a surprisingly strength and pulled him around so the two men stared at each other while Anders looked on. "Her parents are never home. It's just her and me. Please bring her home safe."

Touched, North nodded. "You know I'll do my best."

At that, the tension eased on Charles's shoulders and face. "And, with her, that's about all you can do because you're right. She'll do what she thinks she needs to do, regardless of whatever instructions she's been given."

Anders snorted, leaving the kitchen first.

North was right behind him, already heading toward the front door. "I'll keep that in mind," he called out. It wasn't anything he hadn't already learned about Nikki. He admired that trait—unless it interfered with his orders.

Outside she brought the car around. They got in, North in the front, Anders in the back. There was complete silence while she drove through the city toward the warehouse district. She glanced over at North once. "Don't you have research to do or something? You're just sitting there, silent."

"I'm analyzing things in my head," he said calmly. "There's no way to know what we'll find, so I'd like to be prepared."

"Sitting quietly in the darkness prepares you?" She sounded doubtful. He couldn't blame her. Many competitors did something like he did though.

"What are you, some kind of special warrior who needs a moment before going into battle?"

Her question startled a laugh out of him. "Maybe," he said, liking that analogy. "Let's hope it's not that kind of battle."

She caught sight of a bulge in his pocket, recognizing the shape. "Did Granddad give you a weapon?"

He turned innocent blue eyes toward her. "And if he did?"

She frowned, not sure what her answer should be. "I guess that's good then ... maybe," she said with more than a little doubt in her voice.

Chapter 3

"**A**T LEAST I know you are armed as we go into this," Nikki said.

It was Anders in the back who said, "I'm the other thing North needs."

She nodded. "You both move like panthers, so definitely some martial arts training is in your background somewhere. If you're as well trained as Granddad seems to think you are, then there's a whole lot more than that in your history. And that's a good thing tonight. I really didn't like the look of *Carl*."

"And they didn't like seeing you where you didn't belong either," North said. "We have to assume they'll have somebody on watch."

"I hadn't thought of that." She studied the road in front of them. "I think there's a parking lot a block or two down the road before we get to the warehouse. We could park there, so they don't see us coming."

"Are you staying in the car while we go in?" North asked with hope in his tone.

She snorted.

"Yeah, I didn't think so," he said cheerfully. "So we'll take the parking lot, shut down the engine and slip into the warehouse once Anders makes sure nobody's on guard."

"And how will he do that if he's with us?"

"I won't be with you at that point, will I?" Anders said. "And that's the way I like it. I will go in, take a look around, see if anybody is waiting for us."

"What if there's more than one man?" she challenged. "It could get very dangerous if the two of you aren't together."

"We're expecting it to be," Anders said. "But, because you insisted on coming, North has to stay with you. So I'm off on my own."

She wasn't sure what to make of his tone of voice—if he was really angry with her or if he was trying to make her feel guilty. "You need me," she said firmly. "Before this night is over, you'll see just how much." She shot North a hard look, surprised to see a warm glow in his eyes. It was unexpected and so was the curling response of warmth inside her belly. She gave herself a mental headshake. These were definitely not men she wanted to take a step down that romance path with. They were already dangerous-looking as hell.

She doubted they'd be perfect-partner material. Not that she was looking for perfect, but she was definitely looking for a partner, not just a one-night stand. Of course her hormones leaped up and said, *Well, nothing wrong with the odd one-night-stand, especially if you get a trip down this fast-moving train called North.* But she shoved that thought deep inside.

She wasn't perfect. She certainly hadn't gotten though life without a few short-term sexual relationships. But she hadn't gone into them for anything other than the need to be held, to connect with somebody on some level. And, of course, if she were to take a step forward with North, it would be the same type of a thing because he wasn't the kind of guy to stick around.

Immediately the other side of her said, *Sure, but you won't have a job here soon anyway. You were already talking about heading back to the US. It's only because of Granddad that you're still here.* "That logic is still valid," she said out loud abruptly.

"Sorry, did I miss something?" North asked beside her.

She was grateful for the darkness inside the vehicle to hide the rioting color heating up and washing over her face. She sighed. "That's all right. I'm talking to myself."

Anders chuckled in the back seat. "Glad you do it too. We're well-known for it."

Startled, she glanced at him in the rearview mirror. "Really?"

"I think everybody does it to a certain extent," he said, "although I would really like to know the other half of the argument you were having with yourself."

"That's the thing about conversations with yourself. You don't have to share them," she said, effectively trying to buck him out of her head.

But Anders was persistent. "Well now, I'll just have to make some wild guesses about it then."

A little desperately she said, "Please don't." She watched as North lifted his hand in some kind of a movement, like a silent signal, which had Anders subsiding in the back seat. She wondered about the dynamics between the two of them. They obviously were good friends and knew each other very well. But had North suggested that Anders stop teasing her? If so, she owed North one. And, if he got them safely through tonight, she would owe him another big one too.

If he solved this nightmare she'd gotten herself into, the chances of repaying any of that were pretty slim. And how could she possibly leave her granddad for the US, given his health and temperament? Not that she saw him all that often even while living in the same proximity. Then the little devilish imp on her shoulder said, *And how many times can you fly back and forth in a year? Probably more times than you came to visit him while you lived here.*

And she was ashamed to admit there was some truth to that, but she and her granddad did talk all the time.

The imp responded with *You could do that from the US too. Sometimes you have to follow your heart, and you've been wanting to go back for a long time now.*

She had thought, at times, she'd go to New York, but she had overcome the luster of that landing spot for a while. She just didn't have any better place to go. She thought maybe Kansas or even Maryland, although she didn't know anybody in either spot. Her brother was in California and that appealed to just be close to him. There were just so many options available to her that she didn't know where she would like to end up.

Beside her, North asked, "Where's the parking lot?"

With a jolt she brought herself back to reality. She was driving toward the warehouse where she'd been threatened once already, in the dark with two men who had no problem with breaking in if she didn't let them in. She pointed up ahead. "It's right there." She pulled in, drove to the far back and shut off the lights as she maneuvered into a parking spot.

"Are you sure we can't get you to stay here?" North asked, still not moving from the vehicle.

She shook her head. "No, you need me."

"Exactly why do we need you?" he asked.

"Because you won't know which is our stuff and which is the other people's stuff."

"I'm sure it'll be delineated somehow," he said, "otherwise all the employees would be just as confused."

She pulled the keys from the ignition, adding them to her purse. She turned a bit to better face North as they continued this conversation in the car. "We could have asked Stan. He's our warehouse manager. But it's Friday night, and he's off for the weekend. Normally he checks the manifests, sends the paperwork my way, then arranges delivery to the customers."

"So who checked off this excess shipment? And, if it was Stan, why wasn't he alerted to it?"

"That's a good question. I did ask him, but he had to take off right away. He told me that he'd get back to me. I never really got a chance to ask him again. But I presume because the Only the Best company always orders thirty cases, they assumed it was a second thirty this time. I just figured someone messed up somewhere."

"Obviously somebody did," North said. "The question is who and on which side."

"I want to know what's inside those boxes," she said in a hard voice. "I want to confirm that whatever is being imported and exported is completely legal."

"Do these come in trucks across the channel, or are they shipped over some other way?"

"Trucks. And we do a ton of paperwork to get it all to happen free and clear. This Brexit stuff will be a nightmare of paperwork for us. So, at the moment, it's all still operating the same way. If England does eventually leave the EU, I'm sure the paperwork will be completely messed up for a while. But our company won't be in business by then." She stared at North. "How long will we wait here? This isn't what we came for."

He looked at her and smiled, his white teeth flashing in

the darkness. In a gentle voice he said, "We're waiting for Anders to get back and to tell us the coast is clear."

Startled, she turned to look behind her into the back seat, but it was empty. She twisted to look at North again. "I didn't even hear him leave."

North nodded. "Anders is like that. He's very good at his job. And so am I."

She sagged back into the driver's seat, wondering when Anders could possibly have exited the vehicle without her knowing. "The interior light didn't turn on."

"No, it didn't," he said. "I disabled it while you were driving."

She shot him another look. "I didn't see you do that either," she said quietly.

He held up a small machine in his hand. "With these new vehicles it's more computer codes than anything overtly physical. I'll fix it once we're out of here. But, if we had opened the door, somebody would have noticed the light when we arrived."

"We're still blocks away," she protested. "Otherwise what was the point of stopping here?"

"We were likely already being watched when we turned the corner back there, as it is a straight shot from there to the warehouse. So, as long as we're just sitting here, people are likely to think we came here to hang out together."

She gave a violent head shake. "No way we would use this as a necking point if you were a local. This is not a good area of town."

"You mean, to cuddle?" He pivoted, snagged her in his arms and half dragged her until she was sitting in his lap. "That's an excellent idea."

She gasped and tried to wiggle away.

He whispered, "Don't. We are being watched. You need to know that." She didn't need to know it would either be Anders or MI6.

She sagged against North, wrapped her arms around his chest and asked, "Are you sure?"

"Very sure," he said. And he kissed her.

OF COURSE HE didn't have to kiss her like that, but, since he had wanted to since he had first met her, it had seemed the perfect opportunity to get a taste. As she leaned completely subdued in his arms, he gently smoothed her bottom lip with his index finger. "You're beautiful like this," he whispered.

Her eyes flew open, but, in the darkness of the interior of the car, it was almost impossible to read her gaze. There was definitely befuddlement, bewilderment, interest and curiosity.

He could work with those. He leaned over, kissed the tip of her nose and whispered, "Anders will be here in a few seconds."

Her eyebrow rose. "How can you be so sure? Won't those in the warehouse see him?"

North's lips kicked up at the corners. "Either he's waiting for them to move, or he's taking them out."

Instantly her face showed distress.

He shook his head. "We don't kill unless we absolutely have to, to defend ourselves."

The slight tensing of her muscles eased, and she nodded. "Glad to hear that."

Outside was the sound of a hawk crying overhead. North nodded. "It's clear to go."

He gently eased opened the door and helped her to

stand, though she was still half twisted in his lap. Once she was on her feet again, he stood and closed the car door quietly. There was barely a *snick*. He grasped her hand and walked slowly but with purpose. He headed toward the warehouse.

"How did you know where it's located?"

He figured she must still be out of it from the kiss, something that made him feel good. It would probably distress her to know his reply. But he answered honestly anyway. "Google Maps."

There was a startled moment, and then she nodded. "Right. I should have guessed that."

He squeezed her fingers gently. "No need to. It's the details we take care of." He studied the opposite side of the street and the area ahead. There was no sign of anyone.

At the warehouse, she said, "There's a door on the side that we'll come to first."

As they came up to the side of the building, he was already moving her gently toward the door. "Did you bring your keys?"

She nodded and pulled out a key.

At the door he waited, his gaze searching the surrounding area while she unlocked the door. He glanced down at her. "Any security?"

She shook her head. "No, nothing more than the normal as in a simple alarm system only."

He frowned and stepped inside behind her. As she was about to stride across the room, he grabbed her hand and pulled her back against him. He closed the door gently behind him and locked it. He didn't want anyone else coming in without him knowing. He glanced around to see what he could from his position by the door, but there was literally nothing. This whole area at the front of the warehouse was empty and wide open. He leaned toward her and whispered, "Now let's move, soundlessly, please."

They stepped as quietly as possible across to the hallway with offices on both sides. He could see different company names on either side. He and Nikki came to a large area where the warehouse opened up into a wide cavern in front of them. One side was full of shelving. Large crates were stacked up in the center; then a space opened off to the left. It appeared to have more shelving. It was a little hard to see in the gloom.

She turned and headed to the right. As he assessed the volume of space in the warehouse, he realized the second business probably had more than two-thirds of the whole space. Following her, she walked down six rows before she turned and headed toward the center of the warehouse. He noted boxes and crates and packages. There seemed to be a fairly organized system in place, everything marked in general, like in a library. The shelving had labels, but he hadn't seen a computerized system or even an old-style card-catalogue system. In the center, she stopped and motioned in front of her.

He stepped up to her side to see crates, literally dozens and dozens of crates. He pulled out his cell phone, turned on his flashlight, holding it up against the crates. He read the sending company names and the company names for the deliveries. Each one had a bill of sale attached to the top.

"These were the crates. I opened two of them," she murmured, moving along as if looking for the couple she had opened. She stopped in front of him. "These two."

He stepped up to her side and gave her the flashlight to hold. He lifted the lid off the crate. On the top, bottles of wine nestled inside some kind of packing material.

In a low voice, she added, "If you go below this top layer, there's something else."

He lifted out several bottles. He didn't have to go down too far to feel a heavier cardboard, or very thin plywood sheet, separating the top layer of bottles from whatever was beneath. He lifted up one corner, and they peered in with the flashlight. He couldn't see what it was. He reached down with a hand and pulled out a small box. He lifted it through the small opening, and, with her holding the flashlight, he took a look. Inside appeared to be syringes and medication ampules. He stared at it, then whispered, "Bingo."

He quickly stuffed it into his pocket, and, with her assistance, lifted the corner back up and shuffled the boxes underneath so the space where the one had been removed didn't appear to be missing. Then he carefully replaced the wine on the top and then the lid.

The sound of voices coming from one end of the large room reached North and Nikki. North took the phone from her, shut off the flashlight and pocketed it as he brought her down, crouched beside him. He listened to pinpoint where the voices came from, discovering they were coming the same way that North and Nikki had come in. Of course the newcomers had come in the side door with a key, apparently.

North quickly maneuvered Nikki around to the far end of the shelves and back up the other side where he could barely see through the shelving to where the crates were. He wanted to see who was coming and where they were going. He suspected their destination was the crates, but it was possible they were smuggling more than just whatever this medication was.

The two male voices continued to speak, but they were

now close enough that North could hear their discussion.

"I tell you—she's trouble."

North glanced at Nikki, a question in his eyes. She had her eyes closed as if listening intently.

"But you said she didn't get into anything."

Nikki straightened, rose on her tiptoes and whispered into his ear, "I think that's Carl and Phillip."

"No, I don't think so. She was checking a bottle of wine, comparing it to her list."

"How did we end up with a double shipment this time?" Carl said in anger. "A mistake like this is unacceptable."

"Hey, I agree with you. We have to move it soon, and then we must get the paperwork changed. That shouldn't be too hard if there's no product to match the paperwork. We can just slip in a new manifest."

"I don't know. That might be a little harder to do than you expect."

The men turned down the aisle, coming toward the crates. Hidden one aisle over, North and Nikki could now see and hear them clearly. "Doesn't matter. This double shipment needs to move before anyone else finds out. Thirty cases every three months is the maximum. That's the setup, and so far it's worked like clockwork. I have no clue what happened this time, but we need to fix it fast. We can't have London Emporium knowing what we're doing with their shipments. Go get the forklift, will you?"

"Don't have to. Willy is coming with that."

In the distance North and Nikki could hear a small vehicle. Only it was coming up on the side where Willy could easily see North and Nikki if the headlights shone in their direction. Even if Willy happened to look down the aisle, their silhouettes would be obvious. Making a fast decision,

North tucked her into a spot on one of the shelves down below. The men were still talking, but they didn't appear to hear her as she sneaked into her hiding place. In North's case, all he could do was flatten against the shelving. Thankfully the forklift trundled on by and turned down the aisle to where the men were waiting.

"Okay, let's get this shipment. As we go, I'll have you count them off. We'll get them all out to the truck in the back."

"Sure, but have we got a place for them to go for the night?"

"Yeah, the buyer is waiting for them. He's not happy about it, but our choices were limited."

"Okay, Carl, if you say so," Phillip said doubtfully. "I sure hope that girl really didn't see anything."

"You said she didn't," Carl said, his voice rising. "What the hell, Phillip? Did she, or didn't she?"

"No, she didn't," Phillip said, changing his tone. "It's just that we've never had anything go wrong before."

"And nothing else will go wrong either," Carl said firmly.

At that point, the men were helping as the first of several pallets were picked up by the forklift and moved down to the end of the shelving units and around the corner. In a short amount of time, one of the stacks of crates was gone.

Motioning for her, North and Nikki slid silently forward, across to another aisle. The farther away, the better, as far as he was concerned. What he really wanted was to see what truck they were putting the goods into so North could track it. He didn't have a tracker on him unfortunately, but, if he at least got a license plate, they could check the CTV cameras around the city and see where the vehicle went.

Moving through the shelves the same way they had up until now, they made it to the back door where the double loading doors at a dock were open. Moonlight shone in. He watched as the forklift slowly raised a single pallet and put it on the truck, shoving each one a little bit farther back before pulling out and returning to the staging area to pick up the next crate.

He tugged Nikki by the hand and whispered, "Come on."

With it all clear, they raced to the back of the truck. North took a snapshot of the rear license plate, and he then ran around to the front of the truck and took another photo, in case these guys were using a dual set of plates. He'd have done a lot for a tracker right now. Just then Anders, with a hawk's cry, had him running to the corner of the building with Nikki in tow. There Anders waited for them.

"We need to track that vehicle," North whispered to Anders.

Anders nodded and disappeared.

North watched him as he approached the truck, did something, then raced back toward them. He wrapped an arm around each of their backs, pushing them quickly forward. They crossed the street and strode up the block into the alleyway as fast as possible, so nobody could see them.

When it was safe, Nikki asked, "What did you do?"

He motioned to North. "Track my phone."

And North understood. With a big grin, he nodded. "Now *that* we can do."

Chapter 4

S HE NEVER WOULD have considered leaving a phone in the vehicle so they could track it. And showed the vast difference between their life experience and hers.

"It was a burner. I had yet to use it, so it was clean." At Nikki's curious gaze, he added, "We always carry a burner on us, in case a witness needs to contact us or even a snitch. Sometimes we need it to call in a murder so we don't get tied up with needless paperwork involving the local cops. Unless it happens to be related to our current assignment of course."

That was such a brilliant idea. Hopefully one she'd never have to use again.

Back in her car now, with Nikki in the back seat this time as both guys were in the front. North was prepared to drive, and they were still sitting in the parking lot, waiting for the smugglers' vehicle to move.

"What if it doesn't go anywhere tonight?" She was stretched out in the back seat, and, now that the immediate danger was over, she could feel the fatigue pulling at her as the adrenaline in her body had been expended.

"I don't think that'll be an option on their part. An extra shipment has to be moved. Otherwise it'll raise suspicions. In our case it already has." He looked over at Anders. "Right?"

Anders gave a feral grin. "Right. And we need to talk to your warehouse manager as soon as possible. We need to know what he knows."

"He won't be involved, if that's what you're implying," she snapped.

Silence reigned. But she wasn't fooled. They'd think what they wanted until they cleared everyone who worked for her company. She leaned forward between the two seats. "Did you figure out what it was?"

"It's definitely drugs. I just don't know what kind." North was busy taking photographs of each side of the needles separately in the kit. "There's no labeling on this. That's what worries me."

"Which means, we'll have to get it tested," Anders said.

"And that means, it's all the same drug, so they can slap a label on everything all at once." North stopped taking photos and shifted back to the onscreen map.

"That would have to be machined because you don't want to do all thirty cases by hand. That would take days," she said.

The two men looked at each other and twisted toward her. North asked, "Isn't there a tape-gun labeler where you can affix all the same information really fast, like a nail gun? You just slap it onto each box?"

She frowned, then nodded slowly. "There is something like that. I guess that's probably a faster manual method."

Just then the map shifted on the phone in North's hand. "He's on the move," North said excitedly.

"Which way is it going?" She moved a bit closer and peered over his shoulder to look down at his phone.

"It's heading away from us." He turned on the engine and, taking what appeared to be a completely backward route, went around several blocks, and came up several blocks behind the truck. But because they were tracking it, he could keep the truck ahead of him and stay out of sight.

"It never occurred to me to do something like this," she said. "This is really a brilliant idea."

"Not necessarily," Anders said, "because, if they found the phone before they left, it could be in somebody else's vehicle, and we could be on a wild goose chase right now. Plus we would have tipped them off."

At that she sat back. "Well, let's hope the driver takes us to the destination we want to go, and this can be all put to rest tonight."

"I highly doubt it."

North's phone rang just then. He sighed. "Of course he's got perfect timing." He put it on Speakerphone. "Jonas, how are you?"

"Looking for that follow-up. What are you two up to?"

"What makes you think we're up to anything?"

"Because we're MI6, and I can tell where you are right now."

"In that case, you need to be aware that a truck"—he gave him the license plate number—"is heading out with a major delivery, what can only be drugs of some kind. But whether medicinal or opioid drugs, I don't know. Not bricks but ampules and syringes."

Jonas said, "What are you talking about?"

North quickly filled him in and said, "I'll send you the photos of what we've got. I think the contents of these syringes and bottles need to be tested."

"Send me what you've got."

North handed the phone to Anders so he could send the photos to Jonas which North continued to drive.

"Where do you think the truck is right now?"

"I can see it. It's heading north on Waldorf. We've been

driving away from the warehouse and trying to stay just a couple blocks behind it."

"How are you tracking it?" The suspicion was heavy in Jonas's voice.

"Anders tossed his phone inside. We're tracking his phone."

"Smart," Jonas said in a begrudging voice. "Okay. I got your photos. Now I need to get these pictures to somebody who can tell me something. About how many samples did you pick up?"

"How do you know we picked up anything?" Anders said from beside North in the front seat.

"Because I know the kind of guys you are. One box or more?"

"Only one box. We were afraid, if we took more than that, they would get suspicious that somebody had been into the product."

"Right. I'm sending a vehicle to take over the tracking. I want you to hand over the samples you picked up."

NORTH KEPT AN eye on the road while listening to Jonas as he talked to somebody in the background.

"Scratch that. I'm coming myself. I don't know what the hell you guys have found, but, if we've got some smuggling going on, I'm on it."

"It's hardly your deal," North said. "I thought you were more into shootings."

Jonas snorted. "I don't get that luxury. Drugs are bad news for everybody. Be there in five. You'll know when I arrive."

Nikki leaned forward and asked, "What does he mean,

you'll know when I arrive?"

The two men looked at each other and shrugged. "MI6 likes to think they're subtle. But, in actuality, they're the opposite of subtle."

She watched nervously as they drove ahead. "Can he really come in and just pick up the tail? What about us at that point?"

"We'll probably get shipped home with a *Thank you very much. This is our business. Butt out,*" Anders said.

"Well, that's not good enough," she exclaimed. "We've gone to a lot of trouble to get this. We need to know exactly what's going on."

"Sure, but you do understand what MI6 is, right?"

"That's international terrorist shit. Why don't we have MI5? Involve them too," she said mutinously.

Anders chuckled. "Well, when MI6 gets here, you can ask them that. They can fight over jurisdiction. What we want is to make sure you're no longer in trouble."

"If the smugglers get taken down by MI6, you know they'll make a direct correlation with my visit on Thursday to the takedown Friday night," she snapped. "So, not only am I *not* out of danger, I'm in way worse danger."

There was silence inside the vehicle as the two men digested that. "She makes a valid point," North said.

"We can tell Jonas. He'll want the whole story anyway."

"He has really shitty timing," North said. "I would have given anything to have had him not call tonight."

"What do you think tipped him off?"

"No clue," North said. "But they are always watching …"

"Why the hell would your faces trigger MI6 involvement?"

The two men just looked at each other and stayed quiet.

"Right, more secrets. More shit to hide from me." She groaned. "Whatever."

"When we came off the airplane, your grandfather's driver took us directly to MI6. He'd been told to bring us there first, before we could see your granddad. We were given a pretty hefty warning then. I imagine that, ever since then, Jonas has kept tabs on us."

She gasped. "Really? Right from the airport?"

"Exactly, right from the airport. Not only did they know where and when we were flying in, they knew when we cleared security, and I believe they've known exactly where we've been every moment of the day since."

She was astonished and horrified. "But I thought we were innocent until proven guilty."

"Where the hell did you get that lie from?" North asked humorously. "When it comes to terrorism and smugglers, you can bet you're guilty until you're proven innocent."

"Will we be in trouble for tonight's events then?" she asked, her stomach sinking.

"I doubt it," North said. "Because, of all the things MI6 is good at, it's making scenarios like this one disappear permanently."

Chapter 5

NIKKI HATED TO hear the behind-the-scene details of MI6. It was reassuring but also scary. She'd heard all kinds of nightmare stories about secret government activities, but it was different when it was in the fantastical region of far distant news rather than when it involved something she could watch while she was sitting here in the vehicle. "How will we know when he arrives?" she asked.

"There won't be any doubt about it."

Following the truck, they went forward another block. Halfway through the block, a vehicle came out of an alley and pulled in front of them. "And that's MI6," North said. At the next intersection, a second vehicle jumped ahead of the first.

"Why did they insert two of their vehicles back to back?" she asked.

"Because now they'll separate us, breaking off our tailing of the truck," North said with a heavy sigh. He motioned ahead as the distance between the tracked vehicle and their vehicle widened. One MI6 sedan took off after the truck they'd been following, but the other one right in front of them was decreasing its speed, blocking their path as they tried to overtake it. North hit the brakes, slowed down and pulled off to the side.

"Are you just giving up?"

Anders snorted. "It's not a case of giving up. Jonas will be in this particular vehicle. He sent his men after the truck."

"It's still not fair," she said, crossing her arms and sinking into the back seat. She couldn't believe how pissed off she was.

Just then, as she watched, two men exited the vehicle in front of them. They put their hands on their hips, moving their jackets strategically aside, and stared at Anders and North.

"Are they armed?" she asked.

"Letting us know they're armed," North said humorously. He rolled down the window and called out, "Hey, Jonas. How are you doing?"

"Which one is Jonas?" she muttered from behind the front seat.

Neither Anders nor North answered her, but the two suited men both walked toward their car, ... one on either side. Anders rolled down the window on his side and smiled up at the second man. "Hey, I'm Anders. Who are you?"

The second man leaned down, propped his arms on the window.

Nikki poked her head from the back seat forward to the driver's side and said, "You should have let us track the vehicle."

Jonas studied her with interest. "And why is that?"

"Because I've been on this case since the beginning," she cried out in frustration. "You guys will just hush up this whole thing. That truck will disappear off the face of the earth, and I'll never know what happened."

One eyebrow popped up on Jonas's face. He looked at North and said, "Caught a live one, did you?"

She spied North trying to hide a grin. "It's not funny,"

she said mutinously. "You can't just step into our operation."

That gaze of his zinged back toward her. In a very gentle voice Jonas said, "We're trying to keep you safe."

She flattened against the seat and glared at him. "I was safe enough until you guys arrived."

He chuckled. "Let's see the goods."

Anders obligingly handed over the box to North, who passed it on to Jonas.

He opened it, studied the contents, then turned toward her in the back seat. "Do you have any idea what this is?"

"No, I don't," she said. "It was found inside a shipment that was supposed to have been only wine."

"And where's the rest of the shipment?"

She gave him a hard look. "Don't look now, but it's driving away from you."

Again his grin came and went. He nodded, smacked the side of the car and said, "We'll be in touch." He turned and walked away.

She waited until the two agents were back in their own car, then leaned forward and said, "I can't believe you guys let him take that stuff and disappear with it. He didn't give us any assurances that we'd be updated, further informed. Nothing."

Neither of the men said anything.

Her gaze flitted from one to the other. She got angrier and angrier as she realized how much they'd been cut out of what was going on. "I can't believe you guys let them do that. They took over the entire operation. We're out in the cold."

Again neither of the men said anything. She fumed as the black car drove away ahead of them. But North did not start up the engine to her car.

Finally she flung herself forward and said, "So now what? Just go home with our tails between our legs?"

North held up his phone, and she could see the smuggler's truck was still moving ahead of them.

She gasped and said, "Are we going after them?"

Anders held up one of the ampules that had been inside the box.

She laughed, shaking her head. "Oh, my goodness, you two are good," she said. "Now I feel much better. Come on. Let's go after that truck."

North smiled as he started the engine and pulled back onto the road.

Anders looked at his partner. "She's a little bloodthirsty, isn't she?"

North nodded. "I like it."

"Good for you," Anders said. "She's likely to eat you alive in the night when you're sleeping."

North burst out laughing. "Not likely."

She reached over and smacked Anders in the shoulder. "That's not fair. I can't believe you'd say something like that."

He looked around the interior of the car. "Bloody bugs. Who knew England was full of insects that bite. Damn mosquitoes. What the hell? It's the wrong time of year for them."

She gasped and hit him harder.

He shook his head. "Stupid things. They seem to think they're some kind of mighty warriors, but they pack such a tiny punch."

This time she didn't hold back, and she smacked him as hard as she could.

He turned to look at her. "Did you want something?"

At that, North laughed out loud. She just glared at the two men and collapsed backward again. With her arms across her chest, she thought about how infuriating the two men were. Sure, they'd also pulled a fast one on Jonas, and, for that, she appreciated everything they'd done for her. But she sure as hell didn't want to get caught interfering with MI6 without at least knowing what was going down. "Who can we give that ampule to?"

"I already sent a text to Levi," Anders said, "asking him who he might have for a contact here. We need somebody in the pharmaceutical industry who can analyze it fast."

"Preferably before MI6 does," North added.

"Bullard might know somebody," Anders said.

North's phone buzzed. Anders picked it up and said, "Hey Levi. What's up?" He listened for a moment. "Yeah. Send me a text with the address, will you? It's pretty late, but, if there is any place we could take it at this time of night ..." He let his voice trail off.

She realized how hard it would be to get anybody in the industry to take a look at this tonight.

"Charles will have a connection?" Anders repeated to Levi. "*Hmm.* Maybe I'll give him a call next then." Anders hung up and dialed Charles.

She had her phone already out and was calling him. "Bet my phone goes through first. ... First phone call gets in," she cried out.

"It's hardly a competition," Anders said, "but be my guest. Call your granddad."

The phone was already ringing in her ear. When Charles answered, she explained what they found.

"Yes, of course," he said, his voice a little distracted. "I'm looking up the number now. Give me a moment and I'll text you the address. Take care of yourself." And he hung up.

"He is texting me an address," she told the guys.

Anders said, "Yeah, I've got one from Levi too. But he didn't think we'd contact them until six in the morning."

She waited until her phone buzzed again. "I've got it." She read off the address and phone number. "Granddad added a note, saying he would contact them, and he'd get back to me."

"It's a different address, so we'll try yours first," Anders noted. "If we can get it done now, perfect. If not, we'll contact this one in the morning."

When North sent a visual signal to Anders, Anders switched from his phone to North's, typing in something, then snapped the phone into the holder between them on the front seat.

North suddenly took a right turn. She held on to the side of the seat and said, "What's going on?"

"Look behind you."

She turned to see another vehicle had pulled up behind them, fast on their tail. "Are they following us? How did they know we were behind the truck?"

"We might have been seen leaving the warehouse."

Just then the car raced forward and bumped into the back of her car.

"Oh, my God! They're trying to kill us."

North took a sharp left, followed by an immediate sharp right. She looked down at his phone to see what he was looking at. "Do you know where you're going?"

"Not necessarily," he said. "Anders has the GPS trying to find a way to lose them."

She kept quiet because that meant he wasn't following the truck with the drugs. But, given the choices right now, he'd chosen the right one as far as she was concerned.

"Hold on," he warned. He took another sharp left and then turned left again. And, just like that, he hit the brakes hard and turned off the engine, killing the lights. She waited, lying flat in the back seat, her breath caught in her throat, staring at the men who were looking forward, waiting and waiting.

The two of them looked at each other, and then Anders gave a sharp nod. North turned on the engine but not the lights and slowly backed the car out of whatever spot he'd pulled into.

"Do you think we lost them?" she asked quietly.

"I hope so. No way to know for sure."

Anders brought up the tracking position of the smuggler's truck again. With the new path charted, North quickly pulled back onto the main street and headed out.

But she couldn't stop staring behind them. "Who was that? Who does things like that?"

"Bad guys," Anders said succinctly. "Only assholes would try to ram a vehicle like that. Best-case scenario is we would have pulled off to a stop, and they would have raced past us. Worst-case scenario is that they would have hit us hard enough so that the vehicle ended up flipping or crashing against a wall."

Neither sounded good to her. In fact, both sounded way too horrible to even contemplate. She sat facing backward the whole time, looking to see if they were being followed, but there was nothing. Finally, after a good ten minutes, she sank into the seat slightly and relaxed. From where she sat, she could barely see what they were tracking. Last time she'd seen it, it looked like it was forever up ahead. Finally North slowed. She leaned forward, whispering, "Are we stopping?"

In an equally low voice he said, "No, but we should come up behind the truck in the next few minutes." He took a series of turns, and, with the last one, he ended up right behind the big white truck.

She gasped. "Where's the MI6 car?"

"No way to know," Anders said. "But they're back there somewhere. As long as we have the truck, that's what we need." They kept driving north.

"But we're between them and the truck, so that's good," she said, immensely cheered, feeling as if she had picked the right team in this game to cheer for.

The truck slowed. North pulled into a lane, turned around at the end and went back to see where it had gone. There was no sign of it. He moved slowly, coming up to the corner where it had turned. He followed it and caught sight of it, backing into a loading zone. He drove past, marking the spot on the GPS. He kept going, turned around and doubled back and parked in the darkness.

"Are we stopping here? Are we waiting for MI6 people?"

"They're not here, and I don't know why," North said. "But the thing is, we've run the truck to its destination. I really want to know who and what lives here." He peered through the darkness. "I'd like to go in and check out the place. It looks empty enough."

"Except for the driver. We still have to worry about him."

"Right. There's always something or someone ..." North said.

That's when she realized the men were getting out of the vehicle. She scrambled to step out.

But Anders held her door firmly shut. He looked down at her and said, "I'm standing here, keeping watch. North will check it out."

She shook her head. "You shouldn't let him go alone. You don't know how many men are there."

"I know that. But neither can I leave you alone, and you can't go with us," he said in a no-nonsense manner. And he turned, placing his hip solidly against the vehicle door beside her.

She sat back and watched as North disappeared into the shadows.

NORTH SLIPPED ACROSS the alley and over to the street, coming up the other side where the smuggler's truck had backed into. He knew Anders was keeping watch over him as he moved. North heard no sound of voices or anybody around as he approached the truck. He slipped up between the side of the smuggler's truck and the wall, and, at the far end, he peered around the corner. Nobody was there. The double doors on the back of the building were open. He figured a forklift had picked up the first of the pallets and had taken it. But, on closer inspection, he realized the pallets were still all here in the back of the vehicle. He walked around to the side of the truck, retrieved Anders's phone and pocketed it, then slipped into the warehouse, moving along the back where the darkest shadows were.

He saw no name on the warehouse, and it was mostly empty, which didn't help him to stay hidden. He moved along the back wall, looking for anybody or anything around. But nothing obviously said what business was done in this building. If somebody was here, they certainly weren't showing themselves. North skulked along the darkness at the back wall all the way to the far corner. There he heard two men talking.

"I don't have a forklift operator right now."

"Well then, let me on the damn thing. I loaded it," the truck driver said. "You know I've got to get this unloaded."

North pegged him as Willy, if he loaded the truck. That left Carl and Phillip back at the London Emporium warehouse.

"We're hardly set to receive this right now," the warehouse clerk protested. "I don't know why there is such a rush at this moment."

"It's here, and it's to be unloaded now. It's already been okayed by the bosses. So either take it or don't, and you get to explain to them why."

Grumbling still, the clerk said, "How did this even happen?"

"I hate to say it was a clerical error, but that's what it's looking like. Still, the product is here. It should make you happy."

"It doesn't. I don't have the orders in place for double the amount." With a heavy sigh, the clerk said, "Fine. Let's see if we can get the forklift."

They walked out of an office. From a light showing through the open door, North saw them head toward the opposite wall. He watched until they were safely out of sight; then he walked into the office they'd come from, closing the door all but a crack. He headed toward the desk. With his camera out, he took pictures of everything, then pulled out drawers. He found a laptop there, but he didn't want to take the chance of turning it on and getting caught with it. He wanted to take it with him, if he could. If he had a chance, he'd circle back and snag it on the second round.

With that done, he made his way back to the door,

opened the door partway again so it looked the way it had before. He raced down the back of the warehouse to where the men had disappeared. He could hear the sounds of a forklift rumbling toward the big delivery truck.

What he wanted was a photo of the man who had received the shipment. He watched and waited as one of the guys walked by, but it was just the man who came from the truck—Willy, as presumed. North took photos of him. North headed around the corner, but still he saw no sign of the other man. Worried he had come back and tracked him to the office, North stayed quiet, listening for any sound. But heard nothing.

In his gut he knew something was wrong. Or they had an unexpected visitor. A few minutes later he heard a whisper of a sound. He froze in a crouch at the bottom of one of the aisles, waiting for the warehouse guy to appear. But heard only silence again. He kept his breathing steady and regular, knowing something that simple could also alert the other man to where he was. Finally he heard the clerk talking.

"Yeah, look. I didn't want to wake you tonight. But we got a shipment unexpectedly." After a few seconds of listening, he spoke again. "Oh, good. They did call you. Well, thank heavens for that."

He walked around as he spoke on his phone, pacing at the end of the aisle where North could see him but never so he could catch a picture of his face.

"I don't know what you want to do, but we've got inspections this week. We can't have this stuff sitting here." He ran his hand through his hair. "I know. I know it's crazy." He stopped. "True, true. I mean, at least we do have a double product, but it's not like we can put it on sale to move it out. I'm also worried about the clerical error. Who knows what trouble that'll cause."

The two men appeared to discuss the logistics of what to do with the extra shipment on their phone call. As no real intel was divulged from this side of the phone conversation, North left his phone on a nearby shelf, recording the warehouse clerk. North quietly raced along the warehouse to the office, picked up the laptop, slipped back out, disappeared into the aisles again, came out to where he left his phone and found the man was still talking.

"Yeah, yeah. Okay. I'll sign off on this. I just want to get rid of this guy and lock the doors. Then we'll have to figure this out tomorrow. … Yeah, okay. Yeah, will do." And he ended the call.

With the phone tucked in his pocket again, the laptop safe in his arms, North backtracked to where the smuggler's truck was. He needed an opening so he could leave the warehouse area without being seen and get back to Nikki's car.

The two men met as the pallet was being unloaded. North could hear the warehouse clerk talking.

"Look, the boss isn't really happy about this."

"Yeah, my boss isn't either. On top of that, one of the stupid employees came to check it out too."

"What are you talking about?" the clerk asked in alarm. "Are you saying somebody saw this?"

"No, don't worry about it. I overheard Carl and Phillip talking to a clerk from London Emporium. She came to check the manifest because of the clerical error, like I said."

"Yeah, but that's hardly a nonissue if she went to the warehouse. How do you know she didn't open anything?"

"She did, but she saw the wine, closed it up and left."

"I don't like the sound of that," the clerk said, his voice

rising in anger. "Nobody is allowed to open these cases. You know that."

"Hey, Carl scared her off. So not an issue."

At those words an ominous silence followed. North understood how the clerk felt.

"Are you serious? Somebody saw what was in this and was then scared off?"

Willy gave a half laugh. "Look, Carl is one scary dude. He just has to show his face, and every chick around goes running."

"Carl himself spoke to her?"

"She's a nobody. Don't worry about it. Let me get this last pallet unloaded."

The forklift headed to the back. The clerk pulled out his phone and made another call. "Hey, apparently some chick from London Emporium went to the warehouse and opened a case of wine. Willy says she didn't see anything, and Carl showed up and scared her off, ... but I don't know ..."

North watched as the guy nodded his head to whatever the man on the other end of the call was saying.

"I know. I know. To me it raises all kinds of red flags too. You know we can't have anybody know about that. Nobody can know. I also don't like the fact this guy was so free to open his mouth. ... Well, sure, that's one option," he protested. "But what am I supposed to do with the truck? They'll know he was here." He groaned. "Yeah, yeah. But I'll need to be picked up from there. Or could just drive it back here." He paced back and forth. "No. I don't know what to do. This isn't my area of expertise. It's yours. You deal with it." And suddenly he hung up and started swearing. "Shit, shit, *shit*." He paced back and forth.

That's when North realized just how much this had

gone south. Did the truck driver even know how much danger he was in? North highly doubted it. But it was evident the receiver was pissed off about somebody seeing the shipment, enough so that he realized something had to be done. The question was, what exactly was that? And what about Nikki?

With great relief North watched as Willy returned, closed up the back of the truck, gave a half wave, hopped off the loading dock and walked to the driver's side of his truck. He climbed in, turned on the engine and drove away.

North at this point was outside the warehouse. The inside man closed up the loading bay doors and locked them, and the darkness of the night enveloped the area. The big smuggler's truck slowly moved away in the distance. Then a side door to the warehouse opened, and the warehouse clerk stepped out and around the corner, out of sight. Soon he drove by the loading docks in a black car and slowly followed in Willy's direction.

Moving as silently as he could, North returned to Anders and Nikki. "I'm afraid the delivery guy is in trouble," he said. "I'm calling Jonas." North separated himself from Anders and Nikki so as not to be heard.

When Jonas answered his phone, North said, "Did you have somebody tracking the truck?"

"Yes, they also say you got into the warehouse. What's up?"

"I think you should pick up the delivery driver. The receiver at the warehouse was pretty pissed when he found out Nikki saw the contents. And then he said something about Carl having showed his face, and that was bad news. I guess Carl is a direct connection to them. The other thing is, I lifted the laptop from the office."

Jonas's breath sucked in. "You did what?"

"I didn't exactly have time to covertly copy anything," he said. "And, as I'm standing here outside the warehouse, the delivery driver has pulled away with the receiving clerk in a second vehicle behind him. I think you should pick up the delivery truck driver before somebody kills him. From what I overheard from one end of a telephone call, they aren't planning on leaving anyone involved alive, and that could include Nikki."

"I want to see what's on that laptop."

"Yeah, sure. You can, but I want to see what's on it too. We're still here. I want to copy what we need, and then I'll return it."

"The doors to the warehouse are locked, I presume," Jonas's voice was neutral, guarded.

"Yeah," North said cheerfully. "And, as you well know, that won't make a damn bit of difference to me."

"We'll pick up the delivery driver. I'll be at the warehouse in fifteen." And he hung up.

North turned and walked toward Anders and handed him the laptop. "We have fifteen minutes to get what we need off this computer. Jonas wants to see what's in this. If we can get everything off it before he arrives, I'll return it, so nobody is suspicious."

Even as North spoke, Anders had turned on the laptop. He quickly searched through it, checked the documents available and said, "Yeah, everything is in here. No way this laptop is going anywhere."

"If we don't put it back, they'll know somebody took it."

"They will suspect the two men who just left," Anders said. "And I'd say both of them are already marked for death as we speak."

And that was the sad fact of it. Whoever was involved in a deal like this was not allowed to talk, was not allowed to see; nobody was allowed to do anything beyond what they were given orders to do. And tonight was completely out of the norm, and that meant the men had to be silenced. And possibly one woman too …

Chapter 6

"**H**OW LONG ARE we waiting?" Nikki asked quietly. The darkness of the night had settled into her bones. It was starting to drizzle. She glanced up, turning her face into the raindrops, smiling gently as they fell on her face. "It would be nice to get some sleep tonight."

"We're almost done copying information off the laptop," Anders said.

"We should expect to see Jonas any moment. He's about ten minutes late as it is." North checked his watch, then pulled out his phone just as it rang.

"Is that Jonas?" she asked.

Anders nodded. "It will be."

"North here. What's up?" North stepped back slightly as if to hear better.

Nikki's gaze went from one man to the other, settling on Anders. But his face was impassive. Either unconcerned or already understanding the gist of the conversation.

There was something in North's voice as he said in a clipped tone, "Go on."

That had both Anders and her turning to him. They couldn't hear the other end of the conversation, but, when it was done, North looked at them.

"Funny, both the smuggler's truck and the vehicle following him had an accident tonight."

"What?" Anders asked.

North nodded. "The truck did a flip, and the black car behind it didn't have a chance to evade it. Jonas says both men died from broken necks."

"But he was there. Didn't he see who did this?"

"Apparently it only happened about a mile from here in an even rougher district of town. At one of a couple of well-known spots known for real ugliness. It looks like the truck lost a tire, took a corner too fast, blew out a second tire and went over. And the black car went around the corner and also lost a tire."

"Bad day for tires," Anders said noncommittally. "I presume we're talking gunfire, and then somebody, instead of shooting them to make it look even more obvious, broke their necks."

"Those poor men," she cried out. She glanced at the laptop. "We definitely don't want to put that back in place, do we?"

"Whoever did this will be looking for the laptop. But they won't know who has it," North said. "Jonas is only a block or two away. I expect to see him anytime now." He glanced at Anders. "Do we have what we need?"

He nodded, shut down the laptop. When it was off, he closed the lid. "He can take this," he said. "I've got what I need."

A man behind them said, "Of course you do." And there was Jonas, no smile on his face, a grim look in his eyes. "This has to be bigger than we thought if they just took out the truck driver and the warehouse clerk."

"The clerk is the one who made the call that ended his own life. If you can grab his cell phone," Anders said, "you should have a number to nail whoever he called."

"They're searching the car, but, so far, nobody found a cell phone."

North winced. "Of course. Kill him to take the cell phone. That makes perfect sense." He motioned to the building and said, "All the shipments are there."

Anders handed over the laptop and said, "There's a shit ton of information on here. You need to seize that warehouse so that nobody can grab the goods."

"If only I knew what the goods were. We'd look pretty stupid if we had sugar water here."

"Everyone will look stupid," Nikki cried out, "when a ton of drugs hit the streets soon."

"How fast can we get this analyzed?" North asked her.

She looked down at her phone and said, "I haven't heard from Granddad." She called him back. It had been close to an hour since her last text. When he didn't answer, she turned haunted eyes toward North. "He's not answering. Why wouldn't he be answering?"

They galvanized into action. North said, turning to Jonas, "You know exactly where we're going. We need to ensure Charles is okay."

Jonas nodded. "I'll be right behind you. First, I want to get this place locked down." He called out as they turned on the engine, "If it's nothing, give me a shout. Otherwise I'll be there as soon as I can."

North nodded, pulled onto the main road and raced back to Charles's place. "What was the last communication you had from him?"

"He said he had somebody to call about analyzing this substance. He said he would phone him, and then he would get back to me. And he's still not answering his phone now," she said.

Anders, his own phone in hand, was already dialing. "Levi, we're not getting any response from Charles. Do you have access to his place? Something we can log on to and see if he's okay?"

NORTH LISTENED TO the conversation as he took the corners, jumping the curbs back to Charles's place. He wondered about that. It hadn't occurred to him that somebody would go after Charles. But it would take less than five minutes to connect Nikki via satellite to the London Emporium warehouse and less than that to her grandfather's townhome.

"Our ETA to the house is approximately fifteen minutes?" Anders glanced at North.

North tapped the button on the GPS and said, "Twenty-one minutes according to this." He hit the gas, hoping to cut that down by half. He'd feel terrible if anything happened to Charles. They'd come here to help, not to lead someone to Charles. That would open another can of worms entirely.

Charles likely had enemies in a lot of places. As long as this problem was related to his granddaughter, it was much easier to track down those enemies, as it greatly reduced the number of people potentially involved. But, if somebody had gone after Charles for other reasons, the suspect pool would widen globally.

Anders put away his phone and said, "Levi doesn't have security into Charles's townhome. They talked about setting it up but hadn't done that yet. Levi does have remote access to Charles's laptop, and they're working on getting that set up now. It will tell Levi when Charles was last on the computer, but there's not a whole lot else Levi can do with that."

Sensing the fear emanating from the back seat, North said, "Nikki, keep trying to contact your granddad. For all you know, he fell asleep."

She laughed, but there was nothing humorous in it. It was dark, bitter. "He rarely sleeps. He said there are too many bad memories, and, when he closes his eyes, they all come back to haunt him."

"Well, he has to sleep sometime," North said, his voice forceful but calm. "Even if just for one or two hours. And this could be his time right now. Remember, stay strong, be positive. We'll be there in a few minutes."

Chapter 7

N O WAY THEY could be there faster. It took half an hour to cross town. But soon enough she recognized the street corners. As they whipped around the last one, they came to a squealing stop in front of the building. She was out and up at the front door within seconds. But North still beat her there.

He stopped her and motioned ahead of her because the door was ajar ever-so-slightly. With her hands at her throat and chest, she watched as he carefully opened the door and stepped inside, listening to anything around him.

He motioned for her to stand back with Anders. But she refused and stepped in behind him. Moving silently through the bottom floor of the house, North noted nothing was touched in the living room and kitchen. They stepped into the office, and it also was clear. North whispered to Nikki, "Where's your granddad's bedroom?"

She pointed to the end of the hall. They slipped down that way and found the bedroom door also slightly ajar. North pushed it open and found a light on at the bedside table. Charles was collapsed on the floor. North raced to his side.

Nikki watched as North quickly searched her granddad for injuries. She dropped down beside him and picked up his hand. "Granddad, please wake up." To North, she whispered, "Is he okay? Is he dead?"

"He is unconscious. Looks like he either hit something as he fell or was hit." North's voice was hard, his gaze uncompromising as he searched the area for evidence. "Call for an ambulance," he said tersely.

She already had her phone out and was dialing. As soon as dispatch came on the line, she explained what they'd found and who he was. "He is seventy years old," she said, her voice breaking. "Please hurry." She didn't want to move him. She remained by his side, holding his hand, talking to him, patting him gently on the shoulder, letting him know she was here.

Finally the paramedics arrived. They swept into the room, moved her out of the way, did a quick analysis, then lifted Charles and secured him on the gurney and left. She followed behind, not sure what to do.

North put an arm around her shoulders and tucked her up close. Tired and emotionally wiped out, she rested her head against his chest, and that's when she realized another man was in the room. Jonas had arrived.

She stared at him. "Did somebody do this to my granddad?"

"It's possible," he admitted. "But we don't know for sure yet."

"Then you need to get somebody to fingerprint that room."

He smiled at her and said, "As much as we would like to, we're likely to find out things we don't want to."

She looked at him. "You better find out who attacked him."

"Now *that* we will do." He turned and headed outside.

North glanced at her and said, "I'm surprised you didn't

question him on that comment he made."

"Granddad helped many people. He never would tell me very much about what he did, but I know he had a lot of guests here. Chances are fingerprints in this house are of people who MI6 doesn't want anybody to know about," she said. "I didn't even know about MI6 or Jonas before, but somebody in that division needs to help Grandad. After all he's done for them, it's their turn now."

"Charles has a lot of friends. I'm sure somebody will step in. All of us will. But right now I need to get you to the hospital so you can be at your granddad's side."

She looked at North gratefully. "I was wondering if I should ride in the back of the ambulance. But I figured I'd want my wheels, so I planned to drive there myself."

"I'll take you. Anders will stay here to look after the place and to control who comes and goes."

Grateful, she walked upstairs to her bedroom and grabbed her sweater. "This is not how I thought the night would end."

"It's not how any of us thought it would end," North corrected. "The thing is, we were so concerned about keeping you safe—"

"—that we forgot to keep Granddad safe," she said bitterly. "But if somebody has hurt him because of me, I'll never forgive myself."

"You can't think like that," North said, leading her back outside to her car but directing her to the passenger seat. "And Charles would be the first one to step up and help out. You know that."

It was a quick trip to the hospital. She gave directions as they flew down the streets. She didn't think North worried about speed limits. Still, it was the wee hours of the morning, and, although she was exhausted, she was grateful the traffic was almost nonexistent.

Before long they were parked outside in the visitor parking spots. He was at her side every step of the way as she raced toward the emergency doors. Inside she had to calm down because there was—of course—a long line. She waited her turn and then tersely told the nurse at the sign-in station they were asking about Charles Beckwith. The woman nodded and said to take a seat, and she'd get back to them. That wasn't really good enough, but while she'd been talking to the check-in nurse, North had disappeared. She turned around to find a spot in the waiting room, realizing that most of the seats were taken.

Just then she heard her name called. She twisted to see North standing beside a bed with open curtains. She raced toward him and saw her granddad on the bed. He was awake. She burst into tears, sat down beside him and held his hand gently. "Oh my, Granddad. We were so worried about you."

He patted her hand. "It's all right. It's nothing."

"Are you sure? What happened?"

"I think somebody might have followed you to my place. And, foolish me, I'd had some glitches in my security system days ago, so, when I had one today, I didn't check it out close enough," he said. "However, if we check the video cameras, they'll have picked up his face, and we should be able to track him."

"I'll handle that, sir," North said. He stepped back a few steps, and she heard him call Anders.

"Can they get into your security system without you being there to log-in?"

He nodded. "If the system is on, then Levi knows how

to get into it."

She stared at her granddad, wondering how he could trust somebody a country apart with that type of information. "What about Jonas? Do you want him involved?"

"That's who should get involved. I didn't recognize the man who attacked me. But I don't think he was alone."

"No, of course not," she said bitterly. "They need two big strong men against one small older man, don't they?" He gave her a mock look of horror that had her chuckling. "I don't mean to make it sound like you're past your due date, Granddad, but they hardly needed to send two big badasses to take you out."

"I'll have you know," he said with a smile, "it's a compliment they did send two badasses to take me out. Because there's no reason at all for them to think I'm anything other than Nikki's granddad."

"The place isn't trashed, so I don't think they suspected your private activities," North said from behind them. "As far as we could tell, rooms and doors, locks and files, were all still sealed."

Charles nodded, then sent a questioning glance to North, speaking softly. "Unless they sent two men for two people."

North gave a one-arm shrug. "Let's hope that wasn't the case either."

She watched the relief whisper across her granddad's face and wondered yet again how much he was involved in. She knew secrecy was important to him with his clandestine work, and she could understand that. But not at the cost of him getting hurt. "I'm so sorry this happened to you and because of me," she said. "I'll leave immediately."

His fingers gripped hers hard. "No, you won't. That's

what they're hoping for. If they can isolate you, then they can pick you up easily and take you out."

She sat here trembling, thinking about how much worse this could have been. *What if they'd killed Granddad?*

He patted her hand. "Fool me once, that's on them. Fool me twice, that's on me. They won't get the drop on me a second time."

There was just something about the steel running through his voice that made her believe him. She smiled down at him. "You never really left the old days, did you?" At his guarded look, she smiled and said, "Not that I know any details about that life ..."

He winked at her. "As long as nobody else thinks you do."

She nodded.

Just then the doctor came in. "It doesn't look too bad," he said. "We'll send you up for some more tests, and, once we've run a scan to confirm we don't find any internal bleeding, I think you'll be good to go. But I want you to take it easy with that head. You've definitely got a mild concussion."

"Then he's staying here overnight," Nikki said.

"No, I am certainly not," Charles snapped. He glared at his granddaughter. "Recuperating can happen at home. I don't need to be here, taking a bed from somebody who really needs it."

She glared at him, but he glared back just as stiffly.

The doctor chuckled. "Considering how you're acting and sounding, I'm sure it'll be fine. But let us run the tests just to be sure. Your care is our highest priority, sir." And the doctor disappeared.

She glanced at her granddad again. "*Sir?*"

He shrugged. "There might be a note or two in my file," he muttered.

She smiled. "I think there's a whole lot more that you aren't telling me."

"There's not a whole lot more I *can* tell you."

She accepted that as she had accepted so many of the mysteries about her granddad's life. A hand squeezed her shoulder gently. She looked up to see North standing there.

He smiled down at her. "Why don't we wait here until he's ready to leave? We'll take him home with us."

She nodded and smiled up at him gratefully. "Thank you. Was there any update on the house? Was anything disturbed? Is Anders checking?"

"Both Anders and Levi are into the security system. It looks like we shouldn't have too much trouble getting a face. I'm waiting for them to send me something." Just then his phone buzzed. He clicked it on and swiped to the left. He held it up for Charles to see. "Does that look like the man who attacked you?"

Charles studied it for a moment, his jaw locked, and he nodded. "Yes, that's him."

North turned the phone, so Nikki could look at the picture, and asked, "Do you know him?"

She stared at the photo, and her stomach twisted. "That's Carl. He's the guy who threatened me in the warehouse."

"And was there a second man, Charles?"

"There was, but I never saw him. He never came into the bedroom. I heard somebody else moving on the other side of the house."

"Let's hope one of the other cameras picked up his face. I'll send Carl's photo to Jonas and see if he gets a ping on who this guy is."

"We think his name is Carl, but I don't know more than that," Nikki added.

"We'll find out. Once we get this photo to Jonas, it should be pretty quick." North walked away a few steps and then lifted the phone to his ear.

Charles patted her hand. "He is a good man."

Startled, she stared at him and then grinned. "Yes, he is, but, Granddad, no matchmaking."

He gave her an innocent look.

She shook her head. "Oh, no you don't. If it's meant to be, it's meant to be, but I don't need you meddling in it," she warned.

"I'm not meddling," he protested. "But you're not getting any younger, my dear."

"Ouch," she said, laughing. "I'm not expired yet either, you know?"

"Maybe not, but it'd be lovely to see great-grandkids."

She shook her head. "You're incorrigible."

"Not at all," he said with a smile.

Just then a nurse with two orderlies came in and said, "We're here to take you upstairs, where we'll run you through a CT scan."

Charles nodded.

Nikki looked at the nurse and asked, "May I come?"

"Certainly, my dear. Anything that makes him happy."

Nikki wondered at the VIP treatment. Whatever kept her granddad alive and in good health, she was all for. By the time they made it upstairs, and he was run through the machine, checking that no bleeding was found in his head, she was thoroughly tired. It had to be close to four o'clock in the morning by now. She stood beside her granddad when the doctor came back out and smiled.

"Looks fine. No bleeding. As far as I'm concerned, you're good to go home."

At that her granddad sat up and nodded. "Now, where's North? It's time to go. I really could use a cup of tea."

She chuckled, held out a hand to help him to his feet, worried he'd be a little unsteady after the head injury and lying down for so long.

With alacrity he used her arm to stand, took a few hesitant steps and then nodded. "I'm good."

Just then North stepped in the small space and said, "The car is out front."

And she realized he'd gone out while they had been in the CT room to move the vehicle closer for Charles. Indeed, it was waiting right outside the front doors. She helped her granddad into the front seat, then took her place in the back. North never once said a word. He hopped into the driver's side and smoothly pulled away from the hospital.

"Did you find out anything else?" Charles asked.

"Yes. The security cameras did pick up a second man in the kitchen. Not sure what he was looking for, but he was opening various drawers."

"Interesting," Charles said. But that was all he said.

North gave him a quick look. "Anything special in the kitchen?"

"Lots of special things in the kitchen," Charles said with a half smirk. "The question remains to be seen as to whether they found what they were looking for or not."

"And, if they found something you had hidden, how would they possibly have known it was there?"

He caught Charles's heavy in-drawn breath as he conceded the point. "Good question," he said quietly. "I won't know until I get home. But let's hope they didn't locate anything."

In the back seat, she listened, once again amazed at the secret life her granddad lived. Here she'd been worried about him being lonely if she left him behind to move to the US. But apparently he lived a life of excitement and intrigue that she hadn't begun to imagine. She'd known he was involved in something but had no idea the scope of it. Even now she doubted she'd ever know the full extent of his activities. For the first time in a long time she realized that, although she'd miss him, he certainly would be fine without her. And maybe it was time for her to move to the States after all.

NORTH HELPED CHARLES up the front steps. Even though Charles protested and said he was fine, North said in an abrasive tone, "Then behave yourself, and stop your grand-daughter from worrying."

Immediately Charles fell quiet. He let out a heavy sigh and nodded. "I tend to forget I'm not alone."

"Do you spend much time with her?"

"No, she has her own life, and honestly I have so much company coming and going sometimes, people she's not allowed to see, that it can take a little bit of maneuvering to open up a spot where it's safe for her to come for a visit."

"Are you happy doing this work?"

Charles flashed him a bright smile. "I've been loyal to my country and to the cause of keeping peace in the world since I was a young man. If I died doing my duty, that would be fine by me. I have no plans to retire."

He had such an emphasis on the word *retire* that North believed Charles had no intention of not continuing with his work. "Well, we all appreciate it."

"And I know that," Charles said. "I do provide a service, and it's a valuable one."

"Any idea how they tracked your granddaughter here?"

"It wouldn't take much for an ancestry search to have found me," he said. "And, if anybody saw her vehicle here or tracked her car here or even followed her, it's pretty obvious where she's been staying. I'm the only family she has in England, so it makes sense she would come to me when there's trouble."

"And would your name pop up as anything other than a doting grandfather?"

"Of course not. We keep that background check on me as clean as possible."

"So it's a complete accident that your place has been found?"

"I've put a lot of thought into that since I woke up, and I'm pretty sure nobody knows anything about me. This is not related to any of my stuff."

"It would be good if we could completely write that off," North said in a low tone. "If it is connected, you know we've got a hell of a lot more work to figure out who and how."

"If they didn't find anything in the kitchen," Charles said, "then I'm pretty sure it's not connected to my work but to Nikki's." And, with that said, Charles headed straight for the kitchen.

Nikki came in, locked the front door behind her and trailed several feet behind them into the kitchen. "Granddad, you should go straight to bed."

"I want a cup of tea first," he said in a strong voice.

North and Charles exchanged a glance. North turned, caught Nikki up in a hug and said, "Let your granddad do what he feels he needs to do for peace of mind." She shot him a look, and he grinned at her. "A cup of tea is so much more than just a drink."

She studied him for a long moment, and her shoulders sagged. "I know. I could use one myself."

He turned her around and ushered her toward the sitting room. "You go sit. Let me make the tea."

"Do you know how to make a proper tea?" she asked with one eyebrow raised. "We're British. Tea is not just something you throw together with tepid water and a teabag of basically dust particles."

At that he laughed out loud. "I promise I'll do a better job on my tea than most British do on their coffee."

That brought a grin flashing on her face. But she obediently turned and headed to the sitting room. He walked to the stove and put on the teakettle while he waited for Charles to determine if everything was okay. North deliberately didn't watch what Charles was doing. That was all part of Charles's system here, and North wouldn't pry.

"No one has touched anything," Charles announced, the relief and strength back in his voice.

"Perfect," North said, turning around to lean against the counter beside the stove. "And now how about we all have a cup of tea and relax."

Charles, standing straighter, nodded. "That would be good."

He bustled around in the kitchen, North watching as Charles prepared for tea—preheating the teapot, getting out the tea leaves he wanted from a selection of tins in a drawer. When the teakettle whistled, he poured the water on the tea slowly and set a timer.

North liked tea, but he preferred coffee. The fanaticism

that he had seen as so many British people made tea always amused him. When Charles cracked open a large tin and brought out cookies, North could feel his stomach growling.

Charles nodded. "Nothing like action and stress to bring on an appetite," he said.

Still, it was all good news about Charles's own business activities not having been disclosed or involved in this attack on him.

"What I didn't find out is whether we have a face on the second man."

North pulled out his phone and sent Levi a text, asking about that. The response was cut off by Anders coming down the stairs.

Anders gave a sleepy smile and said, "How is everything?"

"Fine," North said. "Did you get a face off the second man?"

He shook his head. "No, we got the back of a head, a slight bit of a profile, but nothing else."

"Let's see what you did get," Charles said. "I won't rest until I have a good idea who was behind this."

They walked into his office. One wall was lined with bookcases, and brocade carpets covered most of the rich mahogany wood flooring. North stood in the middle of this room and smiled. "This is just the kind of office I could imagine you in," he said.

Charles smiled. "This is definitely my space." He brought up the security video and scrolled through what he needed. "This is probably the best photo, and you're right. It's not very clear."

North walked around to stand behind Charles as he flicked through the couple images that caught the man in the kitchen. "We should ask your granddaughter if she recognizes who this is."

"Then let me see," Nikki said from the doorway, her hands on her hips, fingers tapping a quick rhythm of impatience. "I was waiting in the sitting room and saw all of you come in here."

"We were looking for the image of the second intruder."

She strode across the office to stand behind her granddad. She looked at the second man in the image and nodded. "That's Phillip. He was with Carl that night I was in the warehouse."

"Okay, good enough. We'll track him down too."

Charles looked at his watch and bolted to his feet. "Tea is ready."

With one last lingering look at the man whose face was turned away, North followed Charles into the kitchen, then to the sitting room. When they all sat down, each with a cup of tea, North asked Anders, "Anything else show up?"

Anders shook his head. "No." Then Anders faced Charles. "Jonas did come by though. He's looking for some reassurance from you when you get a moment."

Charles nodded. "Did he recognize Carl's photo?"

"He didn't know him personally, but he would run him through the database."

"Good enough, it'll probably take until tomorrow anyway. What we really needed to do is get that ampule analyzed, and that we haven't done." He glanced at his watch. "It's almost six. We could probably run up to that address Levi gave us."

"No need," Anders said. "I already took care of it. When you were at the hospital, I dropped it off with the contact Charles had given us. They'll get it back to us as soon as possible."

"Perfect. Then that means we have time for some sleep," North said. He could feel the fatigue pulling at him. If nothing else, he needed four hours of downtime before moving on to the next stage.

Her eyes barely open, Nikki curled up into the corner of the couch, her head resting on one of the big pillows. "What do we do next?"

"Wait for more information to come in, as in what's in the ampules, and find out who could possibly have taken out Willy and the clerk from the warehouse."

"I don't think I heard about that part," Charles said in a sharp voice. "Fill me in please."

Splitting together bits and pieces, North and Anders filled Charles in on both drivers being killed in a supposed vehicular accident.

"A little too convenient," Charles murmured.

"Exactly. And now that MI6 is involved, we'll have some help, whether we want it or not, to solve this."

"That's not a problem," Charles said. "I'd be calling them anyway."

North looked over at him and said, "Do you deal with Jonas?"

Charles gave him a pitying look. "Hell no. Way higher." After that he wouldn't say another word.

It made North feel good to know Charles was dealing with the higher echelon in the British government. When dealing with so many secrets, one was always better situated to work with the top layer. He glanced at Nikki, realizing her eyes were shut and noting her chest rose and fell with steady breaths. He nodded toward her and asked Charles, "Do we leave her here?"

"Oh, dear. She'd sleep so much better in her own bed."

Anders stood up and said, "Right, my tea is gone. I'll head back upstairs and see if I can get some sleep. Who knows what's coming tomorrow."

North put his cup on the coffee table and nodded. "I'll carry her to her room. Could you come and open the doors for me, please?"

Anders nodded. "That I can do."

In one move, North bent, slid his arms underneath her back and knees, scooped her up, following Anders to the base of the stairs and climbing steadily. He tossed back in a soft voice, "Good night, Charles."

"Good night."

At the top of the stairs, Anders motioned toward the bedroom down the hall. "Hers is at the end."

North followed Anders to the door, waiting while he opened it. Carefully North walked inside, straight to the bed. Anders flipped back the covers, and North laid her on top of the sheets. He stood for a long moment and frowned. "It doesn't look like she'd sleep very easily in that outfit."

"Sure, but removing her clothes while she sleeps will take a braver man than me." He chuckled. "That's up to you to decide." He walked out, closing the door behind him.

North frowned. She didn't have any shoes on, but she still wore her slim-fit jeans with a blouse tucked in the waistband. She wouldn't sleep well wearing that.

Chapter 8

NIKKI WOKE SORE and achy the next morning, her body not used to staying up most of the night nor was it used to being thrown around her vehicle during car chases and intentional rear-end collisions. She stretched slowly, wincing with pain. Her body still felt like it hadn't had any rest or recovery time. She opened her eyes, stared around at her bedroom and then checked the clock. It was nine o'clock. But too much was happening that she didn't dare stay in bed. She flipped back the covers and froze. She only had on her panties and bra. That explained why her back and shoulders were sore; she never slept with a bra on. It was way too uncomfortable.

As she lay here mostly exposed, she realized one of the men must have stripped her down. The last thought she had was falling asleep in the sitting room. She groaned lightly. Which meant they had carried her to bed, took off her outer layer of clothing and then tucked her into bed like a child. She swung her legs to the floor, stood, walked to the bathroom, stripped down and stepped into the shower. Four hours of sleep would not make up for the loss of a full night of normal rest, but at least the shower would help.

When she was finally dressed again, she made her way downstairs, and, of course, the men were already there. "Don't any of you sleep?" she asked.

"We weren't sure what today would bring, so we all grabbed four hours. Your grandfather wouldn't stay in bed either."

She walked over to her granddad, leaned over and gave him a kiss on his cheek. "No, he believes the only people who stay in bed are those who have died there."

Charles protested. "It's not that bad, but I don't need as much sleep as I used to."

"I never understood that," she said in confusion. She walked to the sideboard, poured herself a cup of coffee and sat down at the table. "You would think that, as you age, you would need more sleep. Instead, apparently you need only half of what the rest of us do."

"Did you get any sleep?" North asked her intently.

And she knew it was him who had stripped her down. She nodded. In an attempt at a light tone, she said, "Thank you for carrying me to bed. I don't think I would've slept very well on the couch."

He nodded and seemed satisfied with that.

She glanced at Anders. His eyes twinkled at her. She glared at him. "Obviously you stole some sleep while we were at the hospital because you're in an awfully good mood."

"I'm always in a good mood," he said cheerfully. "Seems like other people might not be though."

She just glared at him and sipped at her coffee. "What's on the docket for today?"

"Relaxing for one," he said. "It is Saturday, so you're not supposed to work anyway."

"But ..."

"But we'll want to get more information as to what these companies have been importing for the last few years."

"You think they've been importing whatever this stuff is beyond just this shipment?"

"Absolutely," North said. "Too many regular shipments. Always thirty cases. It's been going on for a long time."

She groaned. "Okay. I'll take a look and see."

When the doorbell rang, Charles started to rise, but she bounced to her feet and said, "You stay there. I'll answer it." As she walked to the front door, North was at her side. "Do I really need protection to answer a door?"

"I don't know." His voice was quiet. "But you can count on the fact you'll get it whether you like it or not."

She sighed heavily and opened the big front door. Jonas stood there, his hands in his suit pockets waiting for them.

He nodded to North, glanced at Nikki and said, "I need to see your granddad."

She sighed and pulled the door open wider. "Your face really isn't the one I want to see when I first wake up in the morning. You know that?"

He stared at her in surprise. "Good thing," he said, "because I slept with another woman last night."

When he chuckled, she realized her words could have been construed in a different way. She put it down to her own early morning, her not-quite-awake level of consciousness.

Jonas walked through the house, headed for the dining room, as if he'd been here many times before.

Following behind him, Nikki didn't know what to say. When she walked into the dining room again, she saw Jonas sitting down beside Charles. She pulled out her seat, and North sat down beside her.

Charles looked at Jonas. "What's up?"

"Are you sure nothing has been touched?"

Charles gave a clipped nod. "I said so, didn't I?"

"I was sent to make sure."

"I'm sure."

Jonas rapped his fingers on the tabletop and frowned. "I'm not sure that'll be enough for them."

Charles stiffened. "Are you calling me a liar?"

Silence fell around the table, and Nikki realized that was the worst insult somebody could give her granddad. She leaned forward, looked at Jonas and said in a hard voice, "Get the hell out of his house right now."

North reached over, covered her fingers with his and said, "I'm pretty sure that's not necessary."

But her grandfather stared at Jonas, his gaze hard and pinched. She had never seen that look on his face.

Jonas held out both hands in front of him in a placating manner and said, "I did not mean to imply that," he said quietly, "but you know those above me want more than just verbal assurances."

"Well, that's all there is to give," Charles said, his voice tired and yet not bending an inch. "If they want more, then they can call me personally, not send a lackey." He got up. "I'll be in the kitchen to prepare breakfast. Let yourself out."

Jonas blew out a heavy sigh as Charles left the room, the atmosphere heavy with confrontation. "That didn't go so well."

"What did you expect?" she snapped. "My grandfather's word is everything."

He nodded. "And I have never doubted his word before, and I don't doubt it now. That doesn't mean those above me aren't looking for something a little stronger."

"Then they need to remember who they're dealing with," North said. "Because, although they might be of the generation where a handshake is not good enough, his still is. And to insult him as you did, and in his own home too, will not be easy for him to forgive or to forget."

Jonas thumbed his fingers on the table as he considered North's point.

"You're right. I'll let them know how badly they insulted him. Yes, they used me as the weapon, but they're the ones who have to make good to get back into his graces." His face broke into a big smile. "And that won't be all that easy. They should grovel. Sometimes I hate being in the pecking order. It's not so bad if you're at the top and if you get to make plans and decisions, but, when you're down the line, and you don't get to see the reasoning behind the decisions, it's frustrating."

Anders snorted. "Why do you think I left the navy? So many orders kept coming down that made no sense. And because the higher-ups don't feel they have to justify or explain themselves to the grunts, nothing ever makes any sense to us. We were to follow orders without hesitation and without questioning them just because we had been ordered to do so, and that finally wasn't enough for me."

"I guess it's not only the government but it's every military service all over the world, isn't it? We have commanders for a reason, and we're supposed to trust their judgment. But, because they won't listen to our input or get our take on things before reaching a decision or even let us speak up when we see an injustice, it becomes just following orders because we have to. Not because they make sense." Jonas stood carefully. "Please understand that I meant no insult personally to Charles."

North gently squeezed Nikki's fingers before releasing them and rose. He smiled at Nikki and walked with Jonas back to the front door. And she let him. She was too tired to deal with it, and she didn't really want to give him the courtesy of walking him to the front door. She slouched back in her chair, picked up her coffee and took a big sip.

"You're quick to come to your grandfather's defense," Anders said.

"Wouldn't you be?"

He nodded slowly, his gaze searching.

She didn't understand what he was searching for. Not sure why she felt she needed to give an explanation, but she added, "He is still blood. Even though he is capable, he is obviously involved in a whole lot more than I'm allowed to know about. He'd be insulted to think I was worried about him, but he's my grandfather, and I love him, so of course I'm worried about him. And any insult to him is an insult I won't tolerate."

He gave a slight approving nod, and she was quick to admit it made her feel better. She got along with North much better than Anders, although there was no particular reason why she didn't connect with him the same way. But North, well, he was North. Something about him was a little more to her liking. There was this energy, a spark, that connection that was missing with Anders. She liked them both well enough, but there was something special about North.

Just then he returned. He smiled at her as he retook his spot. "Wanted to confirm he left by the front door without stopping anywhere else," he said with a grin.

"Thanks," she said. "I wasn't quite ready to deal with that part of it."

"Not an issue." He glanced at his empty cup, then stood again and walked to the sideboard. He brought over the coffeepot and refilled her cup and his.

He held up the pot for Anders, who shook his head and said, "I need real food. All that caffeine is swimming around in my stomach."

"Good," Charles said as he pushed a trolley toward them. "I took the opportunity to put a baked pancake in the oven before we were interrupted. I made it extra large, and it benefitted from a bit longer cooking time."

Nikki smiled as she watched her grandad cutting up the large fluffy pancake and then divvying it among them. It was followed by fresh steamed apples sprinkled with cinnamon and then topped with homemade whipped cream. "You're such a fine cook," she said. "I can't believe you're still single."

Charles chuckled. "Of course I'm single. You're the only lady in my life, and I'd like to keep it that way."

"Oh, that's so sweet," she murmured. "Does that mean I can travel around the world and leave you, like Mom and Dad did?"

"Absolutely you can. Today's technology is completely different," he said. "No matter where you are, we can stay connected. So don't ever feel like you have to stay in England because of me."

She nodded. "That's what I was thinking too."

"So where are you going?" Anders asked.

She shrugged. "I don't know. Apparently my job is ending, no matter whether I'm willing to admit it or not. So I need to have another plan in place."

"The world is your oyster," North said. "You can go almost anywhere you want."

"I know. I've been thinking about it. I spent a lot of years in the US, and a part of me would like to go back. Just not sure whereabouts in the entire country I'd land," she said with a laugh. "The tendency is to go backward. I've been in Boston, and it's a beautiful area. I really enjoyed my time there. But I don't have many friends there. I do have friends in California, so that's an option."

"It's a big country. You could explore almost anywhere and find a reason to stay or a reason to not stay," North said. "But you're right. It's usually those we know and love who bring us to a certain place. A home is not a location. It's the people who live there."

She smiled, really loving that phrase. "I think that's very wise of you." She glanced at the two of them. "Do you both live in Levi's compound?"

"At the moment. More individual apartments are being fixed up, so there's a lot of shuffling going on. Once that pool's in, it'll be awesome," North added.

The conversation stayed light as they made their way through breakfast. Until she remembered Jonas was supposed to get back to them about the faces. "We didn't ask him about the photos—Carl and his accomplice."

"I asked him," North said. "He was supposed to send it to my email. He doesn't know them himself, and they didn't show up in any databases. That doesn't mean a whole lot though."

"And what about the results on the lab tests? Did he have a chance to get his sample tested?" Anders asked.

"He said he was waiting on the results. Expected them today but has no idea when," North replied.

"And the warehouse?" Nikki asked. "Did he lock it down and seize the goods?"

North nodded. "He did, but they're making light of it at the moment, until they get the drugs analyzed. The owners of the company say they don't know anything about this. They leased the warehouse, then subleased half of it to another company."

"And the company that subleased the second half of the warehouse?" Anders asked North.

"Nobody has been able to reach them. One of their offices is in France. Apparently they have a head office in Dubai."

"Interesting. So nobody knows anything anywhere." Nikki shook her head, her frustration evident to everyone.

"Chances are," North added, "even if the warehouse was leased to somebody, it wasn't in actual use by the named person or company on the lease. Somebody else could have been using it for their own gain. All one needed was a key and to keep using it until they were told they couldn't."

"That's entirely possible," Charles said. "It's easier to cover your tracks that way, if you don't have anything on paper. And they could have done a secondary sublease and just paid cash for it. In that case, it'll be a little harder to track the who and the what."

"Exactly. So what do we do now then?" Nikki asked.

"It's the weekend. Relax, get some sleep. Enjoy yourself. Look after your grandfather," Anders suggested.

"We can't let MI6 take over and leave us completely out of the loop," Nikki complained.

"We'll do some looking around," North offered, "but we don't really have any other leads to tug, other than to keep an eye on the comings and goings of the warehouse. We should see if we can track down this Carl guy back to something a little more useful than the warehouse you guys already use. And, if you want to be helpful," North said, as if seeing Nikki's mouth opening in protest, "get as much information as you can on Booker & Sons and Only the Best. Like, employee lists, how long each person has worked for the respective company, how long the company has been in business. If they've made the headlines, good or bad ... We'll need that to find out who is behind this. Also we need somebody to run a command center from here, to keep us informed on your grandfather's health. It's still within twenty-four hours of his injury, and he does have a mild concussion," North warned.

She snapped her mouth shut and glared at him. "You just added that so I would stay home and look after him."

He gave her a cheeky grin. "And it worked, didn't it?"

She sighed and nodded. "He comes first. Everything else is secondary."

Charles, his voice soft and gentle, said, "Only if you come first as well."

She smiled mistily. "That works for me too."

NORTH LOVED TO see the relationship between the two of them. He'd often wondered about some of these special men who seemed all alone in the world. But it was nice to know Charles wasn't one of them. He was loved and cared for. He was busy, and he had a lot of government assistance on his side. North wondered what the outcome of Jonas's visit would be because Charles had taken offense, and that was not something to be lightly glossed over.

As soon as breakfast was done, North stood, helped collect all the plates, setting them on the trolley. With a goodbye to Charles and Nikki, he and Anders headed out to the vehicle. "Where do you want to start?" Anders said, walking around to the driver's side.

With one last look toward the window, seeing Nikki standing there watching them, North reached up a hand, waved at her and got into the car. "I want to return to the warehouse. Both of them."

"Which one first?"

"The only one we can get into right now. Jonas won't give us clearance for the second one."

"Right. And, if we go in on our own, they'll know, and that breach will put us in the middle of the squabble between Jonas and Charles that we definitely don't want to be in the middle of."

"Exactly."

The drive back to the London Emporium's warehouse was done mostly in silence. Just before they came to the final intersection, Anders said, "How much do you like her?"

North didn't pretend to ignore or misunderstand. "A lot," he admitted. "But I hardly know her."

"I don't think very many of Levi's team knew their partners for very long before things clicked in a permanent way."

"I've often wondered about that. I mean, if you think about how fast some of those relationships started, the odds are against them to still all be ongoing. Yet none of the original couples have broken up. And that's amazing to me. But that doesn't mean this will work with me and Nikki."

"But maybe it could." Anders's ever-present grin was missing.

"You're not smiling. Does this bother you?"

Anders shot him a surprised look as he pulled into the parking lot. "No, not at all. I'd be happy for you. I haven't met anyone who matches up with me yet, and maybe I never will. At the moment, that's okay too. But Nikki does have a lot of qualities I admire. She is loyal. She is steadfast. She is independent, and yet she is the first one to jump in to help protect anybody else, and she is also upset by the injustices in the world. There's an awful lot there to like."

"Are you interested?" North asked, hating the sinking feeling in his gut. But it was better that they discuss this now.

At that, Anders chuckled out loud. "No. She is not for me. She is definitely for you."

"Well, the jury is still out on that," North said. "We'll see how it goes."

Being daytime, the traffic was much heavier, but they still made good time. Only one spot was left in the parking lot, and, when they hopped out and walked toward the warehouse, North said, "What do you think? Will they let us in?"

"We may have to call Nikki to get access to the warehouse."

He pulled out his phone and dialed Nikki's number. When she answered, he asked, "Is anybody likely to be in your warehouse now?"

Nikki answered readily enough. "There could be. Just tell them that I sent you."

"We'll stay on the line when we walk in. I might need you to speak with them."

At the warehouse, they pushed on the double doors and walked in. "Okay, Nikki. The doors are unlocked, so I presume that means somebody is here."

"Go to the office on the left," she instructed. "Stan should be there."

North walked to the designated office, rapped on the door and got no answer. "Nobody's answering the door. Are you okay if I try to open it?"

"Of course," she said. "I feel like I should be with you. Dammit, why didn't I go with you?"

He tried to turn the knob. "The office is locked."

"That probably means he hasn't arrived yet." She muttered about the time. "He normally starts at eight."

"Yes, but it's a weekend, remember?"

Relief flooded her voice. "Oh, my goodness, I forgot. So, no, Stan won't be there, but the warehouse doors should have been locked." Her voice rose at the other end. "We need to confirm nothing is missing."

"Is it possible anybody would have come in to work on the weekend?"

"Normally it's just Stan, and Scottie used to work part-time and maybe still does," she admitted. "I go so rarely it could all have changed, and I wouldn't know."

"Do you have Stan's phone number? Maybe give him a quick call at home and see if he has any idea what's going on. Also, if you have half the warehouse rented out to another company, you know those employees could be here."

"I must be tired," she said on a soft groan. "Of course that's it. I'm seeing boogeymen when there aren't any."

He chuckled. "But now we're emissaries on your behalf, so stand by your phone while we do a quick search to see what's going on here."

"Will do. What's your excuse for being there though?"

"I'm not sure," he said. "What should we say?"

"Maybe as a prospective buyer of the warehouse. Say you were given permission to check out the size, in case it would suit your own needs."

He nodded. "That's a good one, considering the Emporium business is for sale too."

"Exactly." She hung up.

He told Anders what the excuse was if they met any-body. "She had first thought Stan might be here or a Scottie. Both of them work for her company, but she said it's unlikely they'd be here on a weekend. So we're assuming whoever is here works for the other business."

The two walked through as if they owned the place. They talked out loud about the size, volume, space, the loading doors, the bays, the traffic outside, the difficulties with unloading and loading, all as a cover while they surveyed the interior of the warehouse. They hadn't run across anybody inside yet, but the doors had been found unlocked, and they didn't unlock themselves. At the far back were several forklifts; one of them had London Emporium written on it, so North knew it belonged to the same company Nikki worked for.

He walked back and forth several times, trying to get a good idea of the layout, how much stock would fit inside because, if someone were looking at smuggling in drugs, what volume would be required? Thirty cases every order was not much, and that was something else to consider. They must have other routes to move more product to justify this cleanup. North could easily see how three hundred cases or even three thousand cases would be much more profitable.

"Hey, who are you?"

North spun and smiled at the two men walking toward them. "Hi, we were given permission to come in and scope out the size of the warehouse," he said smoothly. "We're interested in purchasing the business, and this warehouse space is part of that. We needed to see if it was big enough for our needs."

Carl and his buddy, Phillip, who now North could see full-on, stared at him suspiciously. He pulled out his phone

and said, "I can call Nikki, if you like. She's the one who
gave us permission."

"Who is she?"

"One of the higher-ups in the company. Being a weekend, we had to get special permission to come in. We
couldn't make it yesterday." North's voice was easy and
relaxed, but his gaze never left the two of them. "You two
work for the company that subleases here?"

Both men nodded slowly.

"So we'll consider whether we need the full amount or
just half, before we decide to cancel your lease," he said with
a neutral tone.

The two men's faces darkened.

"But of course we don't own it yet, and we haven't had a
chance to scope out the volume," he said. "Perhaps you
could show us which portion you're currently using, so we
might see if we can utilize the rest of it without having to
change the existing agreement."

The two men exchanged glances; then Carl nodded
slowly and said, "We can do that, but I can't have you
checking out any of our products."

"Of course not. Trust is essential in a business like this.
I'd hardly want to keep any of our valuables here if I can't
trust you. So that'll come into play as well. Presumably
you're all bondable and have a high security clearance."

The two men again exchanged glances.

Anders gave a half snort under his breath as he followed
behind the group, walking toward the shelving the men
claimed were all of their products.

"How long have you had the lease here?"

"Almost five years," Carl said. "I think anyway."

"Interesting."

At that response the men walked to where about one-third of the warehouse was partially cordoned off. They stopped and pointed. "Everything on that side is ours."

Maintaining his role, North crossed his arms over his chest, studied the volume, looked the space back and forth, and said, "And one of the offices up in the front is yours as well?"

Carl nodded. "Yes. There are two shipping bays which we both use. Sometimes we have to use the second one because it's higher. We do have one truck that comes in which requires a slightly larger door."

North was quick to give him a frown at that. He turned and studied the space and nodded. "And you work weekends?"

"We're here most days," Carl said with a shrug, as if to say it was none of their business.

"We might have to use it almost twenty-four hours ourselves," North said. "Weekends are a definite. And of course we'll have twice the staff here."

Carl looked alarmed at that.

North kept applying the pressure. "I presume we'll be able to talk to your boss about the lease agreement?"

Carl shrugged. "I don't know nothing about it. But I'm pretty sure it's for at least ten more years," he said.

"My understanding is it's five." North's frown deepened. "I'd have to take a closer look at that obviously, as part of the business deal."

The two men once again looked at each other, and both backed away.

"That's fine. Carry on," North said with a dismissive wave. He pulled out his phone and started taking pictures.

The men called out behind him, "You can't take any

pictures of our stuff."

North glanced over. "Of course not. Why would I care? I'm looking for volume, size, whether our shelving and our bigger items will fit in here. I am definitely concerned about the lack of space."

He moved over to the next aisle, walking away from the men, very carefully taking as many photos as he could justify. When he stood at the far back, he turned and took several photos of the room at large, not close enough that they could tell what these men were protecting, but as if to give him and his company an idea of the amount of space available if the men no longer had the sublease there. When North was done, he kept walking around, muttering. He had a notepad in his hand now and a pen, talking with Anders back and forth.

Finally he walked to the loading bays and stopped, taking a look outside. "It's not a bad location," he said to Anders.

Anders gave a clipped nod. "Right in the heart of the industrial section. Good access, decent size, alleyway large enough that our trucks can come and go with an easy turnaround space. If we had the whole warehouse, we could do two trucks at a time. If we only have half, it would depend on this other company's loading and unloading schedule as well."

"Right."

They pulled down the loading bay doors to check what kind of security was in place. It was just a locking mechanism that could be found anywhere. North reopened them and then turned and headed toward the front. At the offices, he stopped, tried the door again, but it was still locked.

He pulled out his phone and called Nikki again. "We've

checked out the bulk of the warehouse. Two men are here, apparently working for the other company that subleases some of the warehouse space." His voice was suspiciously neutral.

She gasped. "Is it them? Is it Carl and Phillip—the men I saw before?"

"Yes, it does appear to be," he said. "The office itself is locked. Is there any reason I need to go in there and check it out?"

"Well, you can't if it's locked," she said in exasperation. "If I'd come with you, however, that would have been a different story."

"If you give us permission, then we'll be in it in two seconds flat," he said drily. He turned to see the other men weren't around. He stepped slightly in front of Anders, pulled out his little tool kit, and within seconds they had the door unlocked and were inside. He took several photos and said, "Standard office, file cabinets on the right side, an old monitor desktop computer, which probably is ancient, old newspapers. Nothing much here."

"Of course not," she said. "We're not the crooks."

He chuckled at that. "Sorry to break it to you, sweetheart, but generally the crooks don't need much more either."

"It's a sad state of affairs when that's the truth," she said. "Chances are, they're even smarter than we are. We don't suspect anything illegal, so we don't look to hide anything. But, once you are involved in something illegal, you watch every piece of paper."

"Hang on while we check out the office." While North stood in the doorway and kept an eye out for the other men, Anders walked in and did a quick check of the paperwork on the desk. Packing slips, manifests, manila folders.

Seeing the physical folders, North asked Anders, "Files by company?"

"True enough." Anders lifted a hand and said, "I don't see any reason we need to go into their personal stuff. Nikki can always access whatever we need from the database."

"Speaking of which," Nikki added, "I already have a lot of information. Nothing is suspicious, as far as I'm concerned, which is really too bad, because I'd feel a whole lot better if we could find something illegal," she said with a heavy sigh.

"How is Charles?"

"He's gone to lie down," she said, lowering her voice. "After you left, he look really peaked."

"Keep an eye on him," North warned. "He does have a mild concussion. We want to ensure he doesn't sleep too long or too deep."

"I know. He probably shouldn't be asleep at all, but no way I could stop him. I finished up the dishes and cleared the kitchen. I'm now in the living room, working, with a pot of tea beside me."

He chuckled. "You and your tea." Anders was leaving now, and North followed him out of the office.

"You and your coffee," she snapped back, but she was laughing.

Smiling, he said, "Okay. I'll hang up now."

"So why haven't you hung up already?" she teased.

"There's just something about the sound of your voice," he murmured.

Anders shot him a disgusted look, rolled his eyes, locked up the office and led the way to the front doors again.

"Anders thinks I'm being a schoolboy."

"Well, you are, kind of," she said with a delighted laugh. "And it's cute."

"You think I'm cute, huh?"

"Well, that tone of voice is cute," she hastily said. "I'm not saying you're cute."

"You don't think I'm cute?" He stopped outside, his expression one of mock hurt. "That's terrible. I've never been told that I'm ugly before."

"I didn't call you ugly," she argued. "Just the opposite, in fact."

He grinned. In a smug voice he said, "So you think I'm handsome then? That's good to know." He was laughing out loud as she couldn't get words out, just fluttering noises on the other end. "You hold that thought. We'll be home in a little bit."

"You take care," she said anxiously. "There have been enough injuries already."

"More than that, considering we have two dead men," he said quietly. "Keep the doors locked, and keep an eye on your grandfather."

"Okay. You come home though too," she said. "I don't want anything to happen to you."

"I'm much harder to kill than the average man." He took one last look around the district and noted Carl standing at the window watching him. "Speaking of which, Carl is inside the warehouse watching us at the vehicle now. So I'm getting in the car, and we'll drive away to make him feel better. Stay safe." He clicked off the call and got inside the car.

Anders already had the engine running. He looked at him and said, "So is your love life okay?"

"Well, it isn't much of a love life yet." North chuckled.

"But I can always use help." He nodded toward the window. "We're being watched."

"Yeah, we sure are. Let's leave so they don't feel so bad," Anders said. "We want them to relax and to calm down. Then we want them to call in some of the bosses."

"We could plant bugs?"

"We could," he said with a grin. "But in a space that size, we'd have to have a half-dozen and could still miss out on three-quarters of the conversations inside there."

"Yeah, but they seem to have a favorite spot at the very back of the warehouse. They get to keep an eye on everybody coming and going without anyone aware of their presence."

"Yeah. I planted one down there at that corner. The other one I planted up by the offices. So no worries. We've got it covered enough."

North settled back. That was the thing about working with someone like Anders. They were always on the same wavelength because they were both pros and knew the score. Now all North had to do was get through the rest of the day without any more surprises, so he could head back to Charles's and pick up the conversation with Nikki. And maybe, just maybe, take it a little bit further.

Chapter 9

THE HOURS PASSED slowly as Nikki worked away on her laptop. She had some of her own business-related work she wanted to tidy up, and then she pulled the information North had asked for. She'd gotten up twice to check on her grandfather, but each time his breathing had been slow and steady, his color normal. He murmured several times as he shifted in bed, as if not sleeping well. But at least he was asleep, and that was way better than the unconscious look she'd seen on his face last night.

She must have lost ten years off her life when she'd seen her grandfather collapsed on the floor like that. She was still angry that these men had attacked him in his own home. North had said she needed to stay behind locked doors. But she had forgotten to check the kitchen door. She got up and walked around to the back, relieved to see it was bolted. She glanced out the window, unable to see much, then checked the front every ten or fifteen minutes to see if the guys were home or if anybody else was approaching the house.

The phone rang. She walked into the hallway and picked up the old relic of a phone that Charles loved. "Hello?"

"Is your grandfather there?" asked the stranger on the other end.

"I don't know who you are," she said, her voice hard. "And why you would assume I'm a granddaughter versus any other woman."

There was an awkward silence on the other end, then the man said, "He wasn't answering his cell phone or his work lines. I was hoping to reach him on this phone. I meant no insult. I'm a good friend of your grandfather's. I'm fully aware you are staying with him."

"And yet, you still haven't identified who you are," she said, not giving an inch.

The stranger sighed. "That's something I can't do. However, when he wakes up, or when you're ready to pass on this message, you can tell him that I'm looking for him."

"How can I tell him that," she said in exasperation, "if you don't tell me who you are?"

The man laughed. "That's all right. He'll know. Tell him that I called on this phone, and he'll know."

She hung up and slowly walked toward her grandfather's room. She rapped lightly on the door, pulled it open and stuck her head around the corner.

Her grandfather smiled up at her. "Not to worry, child," he said in a low voice. "I'm feeling fine."

Her heart lightened with joy at those words, and she entered his room. "I'm so glad to hear that. I've checked in on you a couple times. And you always seemed to be sleeping but a little disturbed, like maybe you were having a nightmare or were reliving last night's events. I didn't want to interrupt your sleep, but I also didn't want to let you sleep too long."

He shifted so he was propped up against the headboard.

She sat down beside him. "You just had a very strange phone call."

His gray eyes stared at her steadily. "Oh? Tell me more."

She explained what had happened and what the unidentified man had said.

Her grandfather's lips twitched. "He always did like the cloak-and-dagger stuff. Not to worry. I'll call him and reassure him, when I feel like it."

"How about I put on the teakettle? We'll have a cup once you're up and showered."

"I'll shower now," he said. "Then we'll put on the tea."

She nodded in agreement and backed out of his room. As she walked past the phone in the hallway, she wondered who it was who had left such a cryptic message. But the caller had been correct. Her grandfather had known exactly who had called. It made her even more curious about her granddad's activities. Apparently MI6, and maybe other departments, knew all about him. And, in that case, maybe they were also keeping an eye out for him.

That made her feel a little better about all the secrets.

Jonas's visit this morning had been less-than-stellar, and her grandfather apparently wasn't in any rush to mend any fences. Maybe that was good too. Maybe they should wait. And maybe, like Jonas had said, the higher-ups could grovel back into her grandfather's good graces.

Back in the kitchen she realized it had been hours since they'd eaten. She didn't know when the men would return, but she figured her grandfather would need something to eat now that he was awake. She rummaged around in the fridge and found some leftovers. It looked like roast beef from the previous night. She pulled it out and sliced it up for sandwiches.

She heard him walking down the hallway, so she put on the teakettle and turned on the flame underneath it. When he stepped into the kitchen, he looked so much better. She gave him a gentle hug. "I figured we could have a couple roast beef sandwiches for lunch."

His eyes lit up at the thought. "Let's see if we have some fresh horseradish for it too." He searched the fridge, pulled out a small glass container with a little bit of horseradish left in it and said, "We should be able to make this stretch for two of us."

While the tea was brewing, they made the sandwiches, then carried the teapot and sandwiches into the dining room. With the two of them sitting at one end, she brought her grandfather up to date on what the guys had found.

"That doesn't sound good," Charles said. "Whether it's someone using your company or the men who work for them doing a gig of their own on the side, somebody is importing something they shouldn't be."

"I was so hoping we would get the results back by now on that vial we sent in for testing." She studied her grandfather. "I mean, maybe they're importing something completely innocuous."

"In which case there would be no need to hide it," her grandfather said firmly. "Innocuous things are allowed to be imported all the time. It's just paperwork."

She knew that, but it was an easy thing to forget. "I pulled the information they wanted me to gather, but I haven't heard from them in at least an hour, maybe more." She frowned, trying to remember the last time she had spoken with North.

"I'm sure they'll be just fine," her granddad reassured her.

She shrugged self-consciously. "I feel like I'm constantly checking my phone to see if North called," she confessed.

"Young love is like that," he said smoothly.

She shot him a startled look. "He is a nice guy and all,

Granddad, but this is hardly young love."

"I think the thing about young love is that it sneaks up on you and catches you unaware," he said with a beaming smile. "And I approve. North is a good man. I've already discussed him with Levi, to confirm he was okay for you."

Dumbfounded she stared at her granddad, unsure of what to say. She reached for the glass of water in front of her and took a big drink and swallowed, considering what he had said. "Really?" she squeaked out.

He nodded. "Of course."

"There's no *of course* about it," she said gently. "It's not that way between us." But inside she wondered. She really liked him; she just didn't know him very well. They'd hardly had any time together, and, if she wanted to spend more time with him, well, that would be a little more than awkward while she was here, staying at her grandfather's home.

"He'll come back and forth, and you'll go back and forth for a while, until you decide that you can't do that anymore," he said, "and then it'll be make-or-break time."

His analysis was so very clear-cut and simple and yet, at the same time, left so much out.

"It doesn't mean he's interested in me," she said, but inside she knew exactly how North felt. Just not how deeply he felt. "We don't know each other."

"You know what counts. The rest is all just window dressing."

"Is that what it was like for you and Grandma?" she asked.

He nodded, his eyes warming. "I knew the moment I saw Maria. I just didn't want to acknowledge it. And I didn't for years. And, for that, I'm sorry because we wasted so much time."

"It wasn't exactly the easiest of times back then," she said.

He nodded. "Very true. But if I hadn't been so pigheaded and so interested in seeing what else was out there and so blind to my own heart, we could have been together for several more years. You don't realize how short a time you have until you've lost that opportunity. We weren't together for very long before she discovered she had cancer. Back then the treatments weren't anything like what we have now. Not that they could have done much anyway. But she was taken from me far too fast."

"And you never remarried?"

He shook his head. "Never met another woman who made me feel the same way."

"Not everybody will make you feel the same way," she said gently. "But that doesn't mean they can't make you feel good. Or that you can't love again. I think every relationship is different. It's the particular mix of people who come together who make it special. I think you should find a partner."

He smiled at her with a gentle shake of his head. "I think it's *you* who needs a partner. I'm not too bothered at my age."

"You'd be a hell of a catch," she said, waving her sandwich at him. "A lot of women out there would love to spend time with a man like you." She watched the pink tinge his cheeks as he smiled at her, but she could see he was pleased regardless.

"I haven't been totally alone all these years," he said, "but don't tell your parents that."

She laughed, a light joyous sound pealing around the

room. She realized just how little there had been to laugh about in the last few days. "I am delighted to hear that," she said. "And your secret is safe with me."

"That's my life," he half joked. "Secrets, secrets and more secrets."

"I had no idea you had the connections or were dealing with the level of intrigue you currently are living with."

"Your parents don't know either, my dear. Some things are best left in the realm of secrets."

She understood what he was saying. "They really wouldn't understand, would they?"

He shook his head. "No. As far as they're concerned, I'm a nice retired doddering old man, living alone in this house until I die."

She grinned a wicked grin. "And here you are, a Silver Fox version of James Bond, with women at every corner, and you didn't even let me know about them."

He chuckled. "The *Silver Fox* moniker I don't mind. *James Bond*, not so much."

Her phone rang. She checked it. "Oh, it's North." She answered the call, feeling her heart lighten. "I hope you aren't in trouble again," she teased.

"I'm never in trouble," he protested. "But it is good to hear your voice."

She could feel the heat washing up her cheeks. "You do say the craziest things," she murmured.

"Hardly. I like to think I tell you the truth all the time."

"I don't think so. Flattery in a rogue is still flattery."

"It's not flattery because that would be meaningless to you. A compliment is a compliment, and I'm not a rogue," he insisted. "You're a lovely person who I'd love to spend more time with. There. Is that open and friendly enough?"

"I still think it's flirting."

"You didn't say flirting was against the rules, did you?"

"You mean there are rules? I didn't think you followed any rules." Her tone was still light. She slid a sideways glance at her grandfather. He was sipping his tea, a small secretive smile curling his lips. She realized how much he'd already guessed was between them. But then he had made that clear by having already contacted Levi. "You've got Granddad worried. You know that?"

"About what?"

"About our future together." There was silence at the other end of a phone. She laughed. "He called Levi to see if you were on the up-and-up and good enough for his granddaughter."

"Wow," North said. "I guess that's what happens when I show interest in the spy master's granddaughter."

"*Spy master?* That's a really good name for him," she said as she grinned at her grandfather.

He just studied her, a twinkle in his gaze.

"What did Levi say?" North asked.

"Oh, you're worried about what Levi might have said, huh? Maybe you should contact Levi and see if he gave you a good reference."

"He wouldn't have sent me to Charles's place if he didn't trust me."

"Trusting you with murder and mayhem, yes, is one thing, but trusting you with Charles's granddaughter?"

"That's what I was sent for, to protect you," he reminded her.

"Yes, but what about the granddaughter's honor?"

North chuckled. "Love this conversation," he said. "Another one we'll have to continue when I get there."

"I'm not so sure we'll continue this conversation," she said, backtracking quickly.

"Oh no, no, no. This is definitely one we'll have to follow up on," he said smoothly.

Anxious to change the subject, she asked, "Outside of flirting with me, did you have a reason for calling?"

"I always have a reason for calling," he said. "The question is, do you have a reason for flirting with me?"

"The only reason for flirting …" Her words stopped.

"Yes?" he asked, his voice silky smooth.

"Never mind," she said hurriedly. "What did you find out?" Her tone turned more businesslike with that sentence.

"I was wondering if your grandfather could phone the lab and see if we can stop by and get the results. I think we're only a block away."

"He was supposed to call as soon as he finished eating. Whereabouts are you?"

"After the first warehouse, we went back to the second one. But MI6 has it all locked down. It's taped up, and there are security guards on both entrances. I'd love to have permission to go in there, but chances of getting that aren't good."

"You can't sneak in without permission?" she teased.

"I could, but, if we got caught, it would have strong repercussions, and we don't want that to come back on you or your granddad."

She appreciated that. "You could ask Jonas for permission to go in and explore the warehouse."

"We have a message in to him, but he's not responding."

"Okay, I'll call you back as soon as Granddad checks in with the lab." She hung up. "Jonas isn't answering his phone. North and Anders wanted to go into the second warehouse and take a look."

Charles nodded. "They aren't allowed to though. That's been locked down. Nobody in or out."

"So it'll be a little hard to figure out who these men are and where that shipment was supposed to go."

Charles steepled his fingers over his teacup, resting his elbows on the table as he studied her face. "I could get permission for them to go in there. But we have to have a damn good reason."

"It should be easy enough to find something on the laptop Jonas has," Nikki said.

"The thing is," Charles continued, "they are using London Emporium somehow to bring in these drugs. The manifest was for London Emporium, but they were the ones ultimately receiving it. So we need more information on the company exporting the wine and drugs. We got some information off the laptop but haven't had a chance to go through it all yet."

"I have the wine shipment coming from a company in France, but I don't know anything about the company. When I searched Google for it, I don't get anything."

"Nothing?" Charles dropped his hands onto the table and leaned forward. "No hits? Nothing?"

She shook her head. "Nothing is coming up. Nothing old, nothing new."

He frowned and stared off in the distance. "How are they paying?"

"I'd have to confirm, but generally it's by check. The bookkeeper would have that information."

"Who handles getting the deliveries out of the main warehouse to its end user?"

"I handle the paperwork," she said honestly. "Stan does

all things related to the warehouse. He handles logistics of sending it out, bringing in drivers, and he usually loads them himself."

"And Scottie? Scottie is there for what purpose?"

"Mostly for unloading. When we have to move stock, we have to check in orders and ship things out rather quickly. Some of our stuff is very time-sensitive because it's fresh or organic or whatever," she said with a wave of her hand. "And so we turn things around very quickly."

Charles nodded.

"And considering the way the company is sliding economically at the moment, I don't think they can afford to have too much money being lost on spoiled merchandise."

"That makes sense. But it also is interesting to consider that, with the company having money problems, would they have any involvement in this *side* business?"

"I can answer you that right off the bat," she said strongly. "Absolutely not."

"So you say. But when did you last speak with the owner?"

She shrugged. "Months ago," she admitted. "*Many* months. Since his chemo started for sure. He hasn't been into the office in probably over a year. I know Hannah comes in every once in a while, but, other than that, a couple people are left in the small corporate office who run the show."

"It sounds like the business is ready to go belly-up or to shut down, just close its doors, or to be sold."

"That's what I've heard, yes."

"So it's possible Hannah might know something," Charles offered. "It's possible somebody close to Hannah might be pulling a fast one on her or on somebody related to the owner or on any one of the people in the office."

"But what could they possibly be doing?" Nikki asked.

"The assumption would be that they're utilizing the space to bring in shipments of their own."

"Yes, but, I mean, the manifest was for thirty cases of wine shipped, and yet they brought in thirty more. That's hardly pulling a fast one." She reached for her teacup and picked it up. Just then the power went out. Her eyes wide, she stared at her grandfather. "Please tell me that was just a fault of the power company."

But her grandfather was already on his feet, racing out of the room. "Follow me, child."

With her tea in hand, she tried to run behind him. They entered the office.

He turned and locked the door behind them, then said, "Sit down."

She went to the chair closest to the desk and sat. "Should I tell North?"

"Absolutely. Get him home fast."

Instead of sending a text, she hit Dial and waited for the call to go through. When he answered, she said, "The power just went out here. We've locked ourselves in the office. Granddad says get home now."

"On it." And he hung up.

She stared at her phone. "Well, it's nice to know some-body can be fast and efficient when they need to be." Her granddad was searching through the monitors. "Are you checking the security system?"

"I am."

She shook her head. "And how the hell can you do that if we have no power?"

"Because they're connected to the place next to me."

She stared at him in surprise. "What?"

He gave her a half smile. "I own the town house beside us. Of course the owner is a dummy corporation to hide my name from prying eyes. This security system is connected to the power there, just in case the power here goes out. That way I still have power for the security intact here."

"And you did that on purpose, in case this place was targeted?"

He nodded slowly. "I did, indeed." He tapped the monitor. "Come take a look."

She stepped around behind him. Sure enough, there was Carl and Phillip already entering the front door. "Oh, my goodness. They'll be here any moment."

"Not quite," he said comfortably. "They don't know this is an office."

"And how is that possible?"

"Any online floor plans or physical copies don't show this room. And when I lock up at night, I have a sliding door that makes it look like a false facade. It's a piece of paneling that slides across when I push this button." He pointed to a button on the inside of one of the drawers. "At night, before retiring, I activate a hidden button in my bedroom. So they wouldn't have seen the office last night when they passed it to find me in my bedroom."

"So this is what? Part of your spy master secret stuff?" she half joked, but she stared with worried eyes as Carl and his cohort entered through the front door. Yet her granddad didn't appear worried—instead she could see anger twist his features. He might be secure here, but he wasn't happy to see more visitors. She pulled out her phone and sent a text to North, letting him and Anders know what was happening.

"How did they get in?" Nikki asked her grandfather.

"No idea but I will find out. I'll need to do a complete system check so this doesn't happen again. I did a cursory one before, but since my earlier checks didn't point to any particular problem, I shrugged it off."

"I need to tell North that. I hope he's here soon," she said, her fingers busy sending more texts to update North.

Charles settled back with his fingers linked together on his lap while he watched the monitors.

"Aren't you worried?" She studied his face. "You were angry just a moment before."

He chuckled. "I am, and I'm not. I have a few security measures I haven't had a chance to test, so this will be a good one."

"What kind of security measures?"

Just then the cameras picked up Carl heading upstairs. "Is he looking for my room now?"

"I would suspect so." They tried North's door first. But it wouldn't open. They slid over across to check in Anders's bedroom, and it wouldn't open either.

"Are they locked?"

"All the doors in the house lock as soon as security has been breached."

"But it wasn't breached. Just the power was shut off."

"Same thing," he said. "I pushed the Breach button, and the security was locked down throughout the house."

"And, if I was in my bedroom, could I get out?"

"Nope, you sure couldn't. You'd be locked inside."

"Well then, I'm glad I'm here." She noticed her teacup, picked it up and took a sip. "Although it's a bit unnerving to be locked in."

At that, he chuckled. "Not to worry. We can always get out if we need to."

"And how is that?"

He motioned to the wall behind him, and then he hit another button. Sure enough, a whole panel section opened up.

"Where does that go?"

He smiled. "To the townhome beside us. We always have an exit if we need it."

She stared at the door, walked closer to it and peered through the side panel window. "Is it rented? Does anybody live there?"

"For a long time a lady friend lived there. I have to admit that door was quite convenient at that time."

She gasped, turned to face her granddad and then laughed. "You sly fox."

"*Silver Fox* I believe you called me originally," he said with a complacent voice.

She grinned. "And is your ladylove not there anymore?"

He shook his head. "She went back to France. I wasn't quite ready to leave England."

Nikki sat down in the chair again, amazed to hear these tidbits of her grandfather's life. "And do you ever put any of your guests over there?"

"Some of the secret ones." He nodded. "So you just forget about that door."

"What door?" she said promptly as she watched the paneling close and settle into place. "Granddad, you have depths I had no idea about."

"It's always best not to underestimate those of us with a lot of experience and wisdom gained the hard way."

She stood again to watch the monitors as the men tried hard to get into her bedroom. "How would they know it's mine?"

"It's possible they were up there earlier after they hit me."

"They obviously didn't cut the power that time, or you would have made it to the office."

"That's right. They came in the front door. I thought it was you," he said. "I'd let my guard down because you were staying with me for the weekend, so I hadn't thought anything of it."

"I'm sorry," she said. "It's because of me that you were attacked."

"It's not because of you, my dear. It's because of these two men. They definitely aren't gentlemen," he said in a stiff voice.

She hid her smile because, of course, they weren't gentlemen, and her granddad was every inch of one. "How do we stop them from terrorizing the rest of the house?"

"Oh, they're not going anywhere," he said.

"How do you stop them from leaving?" she asked slowly.

He slid her a look. "Both exterior doors have been locked from the inside now. They can't open them either. They're digital."

"And that digital power is connected to the house beside you."

He nodded. "So we'll just sit here and wait until MI6 and North arrive. I've got odds that North gets here first."

"That's pretty ingenious, even for you."

"I've had a lot of fun with this place. It's very much home for me."

"What about all the men who installed this? How did you get them to stay so quiet about it?"

"Well, I could always say that I threatened them that if they told anyone I'd have to kill them."

"Nope. Doesn't fly. You wouldn't kill anyone unnecessarily."

"No, I sure wouldn't," he said with a gentle smile. "But the men who helped me are men with big secrets of their own. This isn't a case of help one and turn around and stab them in the back. We watch each other's backs. It's always been that way. At least it was always the way of my generation. I'm not too sure what to think about your generation."

"My generation wasn't raised in cold wars with spies and intrigues at every corner," she said. "Most of us are completely ignorant of that world now."

"And that's a good thing maybe," he said. "Enjoy your innocence while you can." He reached out and tapped the monitor. "I have to admit the crooks these days haven't grown any smarter. In my day, I never would have been caught like this."

And she had to wonder about that. Because, in his day, he would have been a young man caught up in the Russian cold war and all that that had meant. "You really were a spy for England, weren't you?"

He turned that bland gaze her way and grinned. "My dear, why would you ever think that?"

She shook her head. "Oh, I've got your number now." But inside she was delighted. Not only had he lived a wonderful and varied life but he had lived long and well and fully. She motioned to the monitor. "It looks like they're heading for the front door."

"This should be fun," he said. "Because they won't get it open."

Even as she watched, they tried to kick it, hit it and then to smash the glass windows on either side. They turned and glared at each other, then raced to the kitchen and its back door. The camera in the kitchen picked them up. Just then they pulled on the door, and it opened. But they didn't get a chance to leave because Jonas and two other men stepped inside. And, just like that, it was all over.

NORTH WATCHED NIKKI'S face as he and Anders came into the kitchen. With Jonas and two of his cohorts holding the struggling men, she glared at Carl and smacked him hard across the face.

He roared, "What the hell, you little bitch."

North decked him with his right fist. Carl's head slammed to the side, and his knees crumpled. But the agents didn't let him fall to the floor.

He slowly regained his footing and glared at North. "You'll regret that."

"I don't think so," North said softly. "But you will not talk to her in anything other than a fully respectful tone. Do you hear me?"

The man just glared at him.

North stepped closer. "I have a left uppercut to follow that right haymaker if I don't hear the right answer."

Behind him Anders chuckled. "He used to box. You might want to follow through on that."

The guy just glared at him and then nodded. "Fine, she's not worth it anyway."

North stepped back, and Charles stepped forward from the hallway, smiling at Jonas. "I wasn't expecting you back quite so soon," he said smoothly.

"Except that these two asshats decided to come back after your granddaughter."

"We're just doing our job," Carl snarled.

"Sure you were," she said. "Go and attack a poor defenseless young woman. Aren't you guys big macho tough males?"

The sneer in her voice made North's heart lighten. He really did like her fighting spirit.

But the two captured men stayed quiet.

North glanced over at Carl's buddy. "What about you? You got anything to say?"

Phillip just stared at him steadily.

North glanced at Charles. "Now what?"

"They go back with Jonas."

"What?" Nikki cried out. "That's not fair. I want answers now."

"They might give you answers, and even so they might not give you the correct answers," Charles said. "My money is on *not*."

Jonas walked around behind the two men, quickly cuffing their hands together. He motioned to the two agents with him. "Take them out the front of the house and get them into the vehicle."

With that, they walked to the front door.

"Didn't you park around back?" she asked in confusion.

Jonas shook his head. "We want whoever is watching them to see they've been picked up by us."

The two handcuffed men swore low and violently. "You know they'll shoot us then," Phillip said.

"Hey, shut your mouth," Carl snapped. "They don't shoot anybody."

"No," North said in a conversational tone, "they don't. What they do is shoot out the tires to crash their vehicles and then follow up with a snap of their necks."

Phillip looked at him in horror.

North nodded slowly. "Willy, the driver who delivered the shipment, and the guy at the second warehouse who received it are both dead."

"You're lying," Carl said in a thick voice. "They can't do that to us."

"Why is that? You don't stink like the rest of us?" Anders asked with a sneer.

Carl fell silent. He obviously didn't think much of the question or the answers they were giving.

Jonas stepped forward, held up his cell phone to show pictures of Willy, the driver, inside the truck and the man from the warehouse lying inside his car, both with their heads at an odd angle.

Phillip shook his head and swallowed loudly. "Hey, I didn't have anything to do with their deaths. That was all on him." Phillip pointed to Carl.

"You're in this just as deep as I am, so shut the hell up," Carl snapped.

"If you're in it at all," Jonas said, "then you're in it, and you're in it deep. There is no half-measure here. Men are dying, but what I want to know is, what's in those vials?"

Both men fell silent.

North studied Carl's face. "You didn't think we found that, did you?"

Carl shrugged. "I don't know what you're talking about."

"Yeah." Anders held up a picture of the vials he'd taken earlier, holding it for Carl to see. "This stuff."

"I don't know anything about it. I handle crates that come in and crates that go out. It's not my problem what the hell's in everything. I don't even do the paperwork to make it all legal. The office handles that. I just work in the warehouse side of the business."

"So these crates, are they ones your company imports or are they crates London Emporium imports *for* you?"

The two men fell silent again.

North nodded. "Yeah, you better give some good thought to keeping silent so you can protect your bosses before your bosses cause an auto accident so that they can break your necks too."

They stayed silent and glared at him.

North shrugged. "I guess if they won't talk, they can go with you, Jonas. Maybe a little time will help them see clearly."

Jonas led the way, opened up the double front doors so the agents could go out side by side, and they could keep better control of Carl and Phillip, who seemed to now have issues with each other as well. Sure enough, a government vehicle was parked out in front on the sidewalk.

North stayed where he was, slightly behind the door as the two agents escorted the two smugglers out. They walked Phillip down and put him into the passenger seat on the other side of the car. Then Carl was walked toward the back of the vehicle on the house side.

Just as Carl stood at the edge of the vehicle, there was a weird *spit* in the air.

"Sniper!" yelled North and Jonas simultaneously.

The first agent dropped lifeless to the ground as a second and then a third spitting noise filled the air. His MI6 partner was dead before he hit the ground. Carl's body also slumped to the sidewalk, staring sightlessly up at the gray clouds above. What was new was the bright round hole in the center of his forehead. At the final shot, Phillip—scrambling to get out of the vehicle—went down.

Silence. Four men dead in less than a minute.

As Nikki neared the front door to see what was going on, North caught her and pulled her back against the frame. "The sniper got all four of them out there," he snapped.

"But I didn't hear any gunshots," she said, her frown directed at North.

"Silencer," he told her. "Stay here."

Jonas was already on the phone as North joined him, North's weapon pulled as he studied the immediate surroundings outside. "Didn't you expect something to happen?" North asked him.

Jonas shot him a look. "My men had on bulletproof vests. Of course I didn't expect head shots. How many guys would take out government agents along with their own men like that without even having a chance to see how bad things are first?"

"These guys apparently. They took out the other two in their vehicles without so much as talking to them first, so it makes sense they would take these two out right away as well."

"Nothing makes sense here," Nikki cried out.

"Well, they have upped their game for sure now by executing government agents right in front of us," Jonas said.

Nikki asked, "What the hell is in that stuff?"

"Drugs of some kind," Jonas suggested, "whether recreational or medicinal. Something not allowed in this country."

"And the name of the drug won't make a damn bit of difference either," North said. "Because it's probably just the raw material to be turned into something else."

Jonas nodded. "That's what the lab is testing for. The trick is finding out who is supplying it and who the hell are the rest of the guys doing this because obviously the payout is pretty huge if they're cleaning up and killing everything and everyone."

"What about the laptop?" Nikki asked.

"Our techs are still on it," Jonas said. "Hopefully they'll track down the supplier of the drugs and, if we're lucky, the delivery network on this side of the channel too."

North searched into the distance, trying to locate where the sniper would be. There were houses across the way, and from the look of the bullet hole in Carl's forehead, this shot had come from directly across the road. If that was the case, they needed to do a full-on search, even though North knew the sniper was long gone now. They should double-check that the owners of the houses were also okay, but they had probably already been taken out as collateral damage.

But he suspected that the current danger was now past, so he wanted to get Nikki out of the way. He nudged her back into the kitchen along with Charles. Motioning at her grandfather, he told her, "You don't want him to have too much excitement right now."

Charles sent him a sharp look.

North shrugged and motioned toward Nikki, who was obviously distraught.

Understanding what North was doing, Charles reached out and hooked his arm through his granddaughter's. "I think we need a cup of tea."

She half laughed, half cried. "I think all we do lately is drink tea for comfort."

"If that's what works, my dear, then that's what we'll do."

North returned to Jonas at the front door. "Search the houses across the street. Confirm none of the owners were killed," he said in a low voice, so Nikki couldn't hear this.

Jonas nodded. "We'll do that. All part and parcel of the lovely shitty world we live in."

"Your driver? Any chance he made it?"

"No. We're waiting to see if the sniper will show himself."

"Hell no. He's long gone on the other side of town by now."

Two unmarked government vehicles drove up then, followed by two more and another pair. It was interesting to watch as the British government went to work tracking down whether the sniper was still around. They entered the houses and quickly did a sweep through the entire block. Jonas wandered to the kitchen, to the sitting room, and back to the front door, looking out the windows. Jonas was in his element. All North could do was stand and watch as the process went on before him.

Finally, after hearing Charles call to him, North headed into the kitchen to see Charles and Nikki sitting at a small table with a plate of treats in front of them. North grabbed a chair to sit down between them.

"Anything happening out there?" she asked.

"Yep," North answered. "They're doing the same thing they always do when there's a sniper. Safety first. Check all the residents, look for the sniper. But, Charles, you and I both know he's long gone."

"He obviously knew Carl and Phillip were in here and waited to see what the results of their actions would be," Charles said.

"Exactly," North agreed. "Some things are just standard. They couldn't afford to let either of these men talk, which meant they knew something. Or were at least connected to something or to someone who knew something, and they didn't want that connection to become clear."

"Is this likely to last for hours?" Nikki asked, staring toward the front door. "As much as I want the sniper caught and punished who killed those two agents and to know more about what Carl and Phillip knew, I'm really tired. I'm working off of only four hours' sleep. And this isn't how I had planned to spend my day."

"No, but you got to see a lot more than you would have on any normal day," Charles said with a sigh. "At least now you know I'm perfectly safe here."

"You can't be *perfectly* safe," she reminded him. "After all, you did get attacked and were knocked unconscious."

He appeared to concede that point. "So ninety-nine percent of the time I'm very safe here," he said. "I just have to be sure who it is I'm expecting to come into the house."

She reached for a scone, split it in half and put butter on both sides. North watched with interest. She caught his glance and slipped the thing onto his plate and selected another one for herself.

He picked it up and took a bite. "Charles, you are a fantastic cook."

"Thank you. It's one hobby I really do enjoy taking time for," he said with a tiny smile at the corners of his mouth.

"So what do we do now?" Nikki glanced around. "And where's Anders?"

"Keeping an eye on the back of the house," North said.

"The back?"

"Yes. As Jonas and all his men are busy in the front, we wanted to confirm that somebody would keep an eye out in the back."

Her shoulders slumped as she nodded. "I guess that makes sense. It'd be really nice to get this over with though."

"Absolutely." He pulled out his phone, placed it on the table and said, "I'll take a look at the research material you've found for us. Maybe we'll dredge something out of that section."

"Or not," she said. "Jonas should have picked up whatever paperwork and stolen goods or illegal goods were in that one warehouse. I'm not sure there's much more we can find out on our own."

Charles and North both chuckled.

She groaned. "Okay, so you guys do this all the time, but I don't. It seems like we've done all we can. But you're saying we haven't. So what else can we do?"

"Now we dig into Carl's and Phillip's lives," North said. "They connect to someone who doesn't want them to live, so I need to know who that someone is."

She tilted her head, looked at him and gave a clipped nod. "That makes sense."

"Thank you," he said humbly. "I do try."

She rolled her eyes at him, and he just laughed.

His phone buzzed. He looked at it and said, "It's Anders. I'll take his place outside." He got up, nodded to the two of them and slipped out the back door.

He headed to the corner, walking normally, naturally, in case he was being watched, then, just before he reached the back alley, he slid up to the corner and waited. A whistle came, telling him it was all clear. He stepped around the corner and casually strolled along the alleyway to the small backyards of the other properties, and there was Anders waiting for him.

"Nothing here. It's all quiet," Anders said in a low tone. "I'm not sure what's going on in front, but ..."

"Nothing unusual," North said. "Jonas has teams all

over the place."

"All these back gardens have this pathway behind the lots, not even a real alleyway beyond them," he said, "but it's definitely a place to exit if somebody got caught in this area. And that's only if they didn't jump into the actual backyards."

"Exactly. There's treats inside if you want something."

Anders shrugged. "I can stay out here. I just wanted to touch base and to get an update."

"I'm not sure there's any point in staying here. We have a lot of research to do. With two more smugglers dead now, we need to tear apart their lives and find out who the hell the sniper was, and, if it wasn't their boss, then who's the man who ordered the sniper into action. If anyone ordered this. It's quite possible their boss was cleaning up all by himself."

"And, as usual, instead of getting clearer on all this, we're getting deeper into it," Anders said.

The two of them walked back into Charles's yard and up toward the house.

"But I also think the head smuggler's mistakes are getting bigger," North said. "It's not too often we get the lowlifes taken out by the big bosses. So Carl and Phillip knew something or someone. And now we have to find out what or who that is."

Chapter 10

NIKKI WATCHED AS both men came in the rear kitchen door. She smiled and said, "If it's not too late, I want to take some of my work and go to the main office. It'll be empty, but I go in on a weekend if I have to."

"How often do you do that?" North asked.

She twisted her lips slightly as she thought about it. "Once a month normally. It depends on the accumulation of paperwork. I always take in a hard copy, and I want to check in with the office to see if anything has changed. So much is happening with the owner being ill that I'm always afraid I'll go in one day to find it all locked up—like my key won't work. That nobody would have told me how the company has gone under or been sold or just that the doors were closed and how I'm not getting paid anymore."

"That's got to be hard to work under those circumstances," Anders said.

She nodded. "Yes. It's extremely uncomfortable."

"We can go now if you want," North said.

She looked at him in surprise. "How long will the MI6 men be here for?"

"Probably another few hours, but your vehicle is free and clear. We can go if you'd like."

She stood. "I do like. That would help a lot if I could at least clear some of this off, and I can reassure myself I have a job to go to come Monday." She leaned over, kissed her granddad on the temple and said, "Now you look after yourself. Anders will keep watch for you."

Her grandfather chuckled. "That's fine. I'll look after Anders."

Anders threw himself into the chair she had vacated and said, "He's looking after me just fine." He reached across the small table for a large scone. He held it up and then took a bite.

Nikki sighed. "You know you're supposed to open them, and put butter and jam on the halves, right?"

He looked at her in surprise and then took the knife, opened his scone and proceeded to cover both sides with a thick layer of butter.

She watched in fascination. "You don't do anything in half measures, do you?"

He shrugged and then protested, "First you don't like that I eat it without butter. Then you don't like the amount of butter I put on it."

She groaned, turned around, grabbed North's arm and said, "Let's go." Over her shoulder, she called out, "We won't be long."

He wrapped an arm around her as they walked to the front door. When they stepped out, Jonas was on the sidewalk, talking to another man. Jonas looked up at the two of them. North directed her down the steps and toward Jonas's side. "We want to head up to her corporate office. She has some paperwork and whatnot she needs to take in."

Jonas considered it for a moment, his foot tapping the cement. "Fine. But, if you see anything unusual, you call me directly. You hear me?"

"Sure. But what do you expect us to find?" she asked in

confusion.

"Considering it's your company that brought in these vials, I can't say what we're expecting to find. Just anything out of the ordinary."

She gave a light shrug and nodded. "I can do that."

As they walked away, Jonas called out, "Never mind. I'll send a man with you." He spun around and said, "Dan, I want you to go with these two to her office. Take a look around, get some photos, and, if anything is unusual, report back to me."

A tall lanky man walked to where they stood and asked, "What vehicle are we going in?"

She pointed to her small car.

He nodded. The three of them got in, and she slowly drove through town to where the offices were.

She parked on the street and said, "Nobody will be here because it's a Saturday." She walked into the main lobby and used her key to get in the office door. "We used to have a big office, but now we're down to just a few of us. And, of course, with the owner being sick, if the business doesn't get sold, chances are it'll just fade away into nothing soon."

"For that to happen, you have to stop taking orders and shipping and receiving them."

She nodded. "I suspect that's what the office staff has been doing, shutting things down." She walked into a small room and stopped, studying it. "It still looks the same, just two desks, two computers, both laptops, chairs. Not a whole lot else."

Dan stepped forward and asked, "Is this normal?"

"It is, considering we're eking out an existence," she said with a fatalistic tone. "It's all over with but locking the door."

"I need the owner's address," Dan said. He pulled out a notepad. "How can we reach him?"

She gave Dan the admin's name and number. "She works at his house with him, and we communicate back and forth."

"Is this office even needed?"

North spoke up. "I don't see how it could be. No paperwork is on their desks. What do they do all day?" He turned one laptop around, lifted the lid and turned it on. As soon as it loaded, there was no login, nothing. It just popped up with the desktop, and he checked some documents there and any history of use. "They've logged in like hundreds of hours of solitaire."

"And probably playing games online," she admitted. "The last time I was in here, they said they were running out of work and didn't know how much longer they would keep this job."

"Nobody has logged in since Wednesday on this one. There have been no users since Wednesday," he corrected.

"They might have taken Thursday and Friday off," she said. "I don't know. Things have been a little crazy for me for the last few days."

He nodded. "That's true enough, but we need to talk to them ourselves." He turned to look at her. "What number do you call to talk to them?"

She pulled out her phone, hit a few buttons and a small phone sitting off to the side rang.

"So you're still using landlines instead of cell phones for each of them?" North asked.

Nikki nodded.

"When did you last call here?" Dan asked.

She stopped and thought about it. "I think it was just in

the last couple days." With her phone out, she checked through for the admin's name. She hit Dial. When a woman answered on the other end, Nikki said, "Hey, it's me. I wonder if the guys are in the office these days."

Hannah laughed on the other end of the phone. "There's only one now. The other one got another job a week ago, and I don't know when Tyler was in last."

"Are we still functioning as a business?" Nikki asked in surprise. "Are they taking orders, or are we only completing the ones we have?"

"They've been completing the ones we have, and most of those are done now. Just the last couple coming in."

"So how much longer do we have?" Nikki turned to look around the office in confusion.

"Maybe two weeks max," Hannah said.

"Is the business that close to being done?" she cried out. "How come nobody told me?"

"We thought you knew," Hannah said in confusion. "You know the business is ready to shut down."

"Yes, but, last time we spoke, you said it was for sale."

"Sure, but it's been for sale for months now with no interest. Without any orders coming in and no shipments, there is nothing to sell," she said. "I didn't speak to anybody in the office the last couple days, so I don't know who all has been there. Why does it matter?"

"If they're drawing a paycheck, you would hope they're showing up to work."

"Oh, well, Tyler is only drawing a paycheck for next week. We were hoping you could finish the last of the orders."

"And what about the double shipment I went to check on?"

"Yes, what about it? We do need to get that one sorted out before we shut the doors. We can't have a big mistake like that hanging over our heads."

"Good point. And how is Nathan?" Nikki asked suddenly. "I know you're really close to him."

Hannah cried lightly. "He is ... He is not in a good way. I don't think he has more than a couple months. If that."

"Oh, dear. I'm so sorry," Nikki said. "I gather then I don't have a job at the end of next week."

"Yes. Unfortunately that's the way it looks. I'm trying to shut things down at this end. There is a severance package for you when it's done," she rushed to say. "So it's not like you'll be completely out in the cold."

Nikki could hear the loss in Hannah's voice and realized her relationship with Nathan was much closer than Nikki had first thought. "I'm so sorry. This is obviously a very difficult time for you."

Hannah rallied slightly. "It's much harder for Nathan. He's not ready to go."

Nikki looked over at Dan and North. North was shaking his head. "Okay. Well, let me see if I can tidy up this final issue, and I'll get back to you as soon as I can." Leaving Hannah weeping gently, Nikki hung up her phone and groaned. "Apparently the owner is almost gone, and one of the guys working here in the office found another job, left a week ago. The other one, Tyler, is due to work here through the end of next week. Hannah is not sure if he showed up Thursday or Friday, and I don't think she particularly cares. We have just one or two final shipments. I didn't even mention the nightmare at the warehouse. What do you want me to do?"

"You might want to consider how the warehouse section

that's yours is still really full. What's happening with all of that?"

She stared at him in surprise. "You're right. All of that material needs to be moved out." She phoned Hannah back, but there was no answer. Frowning, she put away her phone. "She is not answering."

"We should go back to the warehouse and take a look at what products are still sitting there," he said slowly. "Maybe somebody else is using that part of the warehouse designated as Emporium's, or maybe the other company, the subleasee, has sprawled their stuff over on your side."

She walked to the laptop that was booted up and looked around at its desktop. Then she spun around and pulled out all the drawers to the nearby filing cabinet. "Even the physical files are gone."

Just then Hannah called her back. "I missed your call. What's up?"

"When I was in the warehouse last, there was still a lot of product on the shelves."

"No, no, no," Hannah said. "None of that is ours. The other company who leases space needed more room temporarily. So I told him that they could sprawl a little bit, until Emporium was sold or the company closed down. The five-year lease on the place is almost up, and they were looking to take the whole thing over."

"And no files are in the cabinets here anymore."

"No, I've gone through and brought everything back here. Most of the files have been closed. All the suppliers and the vendors were told the company is going out of business."

"And you did that recently?"

"Last week," Hannah admitted. "Nathan just wants to find peace by putting it all to rest. It was his company for so long, but, with nobody to pass it on to, I think he wants to know he has cleaned off everything on his plate and has tidied it all up so there's nothing left in a mess when he goes."

After saying goodbye to Hannah, Nikki turned and explained to the guys how the business stood.

"In that case, we need to return to the warehouse," North said. "We have to find out exactly what's happening there."

She nodded. "But none of that product is ours legally."

"Sure," Dan said. "But, if you think about it, at least three of the men who worked there are now dead. I'll get clearance, and we'll go take a look."

NORTH DROVE FROM the corporate office to the warehouse. He'd never seen a business slowly run down to nothing, but he could see how it could happen if a vibrant and strong owner suddenly faded with a crippling disease; then everything fell apart. Particularly if the one boss managed everything and if it wasn't a terribly large enterprise to begin with. Nathan had limped along for a while, but obviously his business was at the end stages of death, like its owner. And it was too easy for others to step in and to take advantage.

North had to admit that he wondered if Hannah had taken advantage of Nathan's health condition and was doing something on the side herself. He was relieved to consider the fact that it was more than likely the subleasee that had been utilizing some of the warehouse space and was now spreading out, taking over the rest of the warehouse space. If there was nothing left in the warehouse that belonged to Nikki's company, or very little, then North needed to take a closer look at the rest of the products there. Were they also fake shipments of goods with the real commodities buried underneath?

The vehicle was silent inside the whole way to the warehouse. North could sense Nikki's fidgety nervousness. Who wanted to consider any of the people you worked with closely were taking advantage of Nathan's impending death?

"How well did you know the men who worked in the corporate office?" Dan asked.

It was a good question. North didn't think he himself had asked her that yet.

"I've worked with them for five years," she said. "We've been a tight-knit family for all that time. Nathan's disease was quite shocking. We thought he'd be away just for a few months, and he'd be back strong, running the company again. But instead it appears to have been exactly the opposite," she said sadly.

She tried to explain the setup and how it had deteriorated for Dan's sake. North had heard most of it before so wasn't learning anything new.

"So you really don't have a job after next Friday?" North asked at one point.

"Apparently not." Staring out the window, her voice was sad. "Hannah might have said something to me earlier, but I could've been just in a state of denial. I don't know. She seemed to think she had. But then everybody has been slowly disappearing on me, so I wasn't exactly trying to source out the truth of the matter. I was just hoping it would all go away."

"How is that working out for you?" North asked with a note of amusement in his voice.

"Obviously not so good," she snapped. "Hannah did say

there was a severance package for me though, that I won't be completely out in the cold as of Friday."

"That's generous."

"It probably would have been a lot more generous if Nathan had sold the business. As it is, this way there's nothing but a small package."

Just then they turned onto the street lining up to the warehouse. "Pull into the same parking lot as before, if that's okay with you," he said.

"Yes, that's fine," she said. "Hopefully there'll be lots of room. It is a weekend."

Some of the parking lot spaces were filled, but there was definitely a spot to pull into. They got out, and he locked up the vehicle, and they strode toward the warehouse. "What do you want to guess," he said to Dan, "a new welcoming party or the building's empty?"

"The order was placed through London Emporium, but then, instead of it being delivered to Only the Best's stores, Booker & Sons took possession and moved it through their own network. At least that's how I see this going down. Now whether Only the Best was the end destination, I don't know." Dan turned to Nikki. "How many men threatened you the first time?"

"Two. Carl and Phillip. I don't know if anyone else was there in the back of the warehouse though."

"Willy was." Dan glanced at North. "And when you came here with Anders?"

"Just the first two men again. At least as far as I could tell."

"So either new muscle or no muscle," Dan said smoothly.

They walked up to the side door. Nikki found it wasn't

locked, and she pushed it open, stepping inside. "If it's not locked, then somebody should be here." There was a harsh echo to the place, as if it was empty. She walked over to the warehouse office, used her key and unlocked that door. She stepped inside. "Nothing has been disturbed in here."

Dan walked around and said, "We might take that laptop with us when we go though."

She shrugged. "I'm not even sure Stan knows he's got no job." And then she stopped. "Hey, that makes no sense." She pulled out her phone and dialed somebody. "Hannah, what about Stan from the warehouse? When is his job ending?"

"Well, the warehouse is empty, so he's done next Friday too. Honestly he probably won't even be there all week because, if we don't have any product, there's no point."

"I wonder how often Stan has been here this last week," she said quietly.

"If there hasn't been anything for him to do, then there hasn't really been any reason for him to be there, is there?" Then, all of a sudden, Hannah seemed to clue in. "Why? Is there a problem?"

"Maybe," Nikki said. "I'll check it out further, then let you know. But maybe you should contact Stan and confirm when and how often he has been in here. And let him know it's okay if he hasn't been around very much, just so we get the truth."

"Stan has worked for the company for twenty years. He was looking forward to retiring, but I knew he would be there right to the bitter end," Hannah said.

"I'm not implying anything other than that at all," Nikki said hurriedly.

North listened to the rest of the conversation and realized just how splintered off the company had been as everybody saw the inevitable end come toward them. North walked out of the office, crossed to the other office and checked that it was locked. It was.

Dan looked at him and said, "What do you think?"

"I think we should do a quick search to double-check that we are actually alone, and then I suggest we open that other office."

Both men splitting up, Dan went left, and North went right, leaving Nikki at the first office.

North slipped along the far right against the wall as he went down row after row after row of goods, watching them all as he passed, going from one to the other. He didn't walk up and down the aisles but crossed at the end so he could see if anybody was in the aisles. Once he made it to the other side, he came along the edge, noting the multitude of packing crates and boxes. He didn't take any time to stop and check to see what was in them. That was another issue altogether. Maybe this company was on the up-and-up, and somebody else was just utilizing their facilities as well.

There were so many ways for somebody to take advantage here that North didn't want to jump to any conclusions. He watched as Dan came around the corner; then they slowly walked toward each other. There didn't appear to be anybody here, but North didn't trust that initial conclusion. He frowned, his footsteps slowing as he came to where the crates had been unloaded.

Dan joined him.

North pointed at the empty section and said, "All the crates were moved from here."

"And the crates aren't small," Dan said. "I saw them in the other warehouse. Any cameras in here?"

"No. Who else is involved in this mess? Maybe the sniper." North frowned. "Did we ever get confirmation that it was drugs?"

"It's an element they use for creating new recreational drugs. It's to double the punch, so to speak. Highly dangerous and illegal in England."

"*Nice*," North said. But in his head he was saying, *Not nice*. That really sucked. "At least we caught it."

"This much, yes, and it's a lot. We've often thought there was a new supplier in town. But we couldn't figure out how they were getting the drug across into England. But, of course now, what we're realizing is, they are making it here. So they're importing the raw materials and manufacturing it in England, where the supply chain is already established. We have to go higher than what we found here to get to the men behind this. And that'll be in Europe. This is just one of the steps in this ladder."

North turned back toward the forklifts. "My understanding is one of these belongs to Nikki's company, and one belongs to the other one."

"In which case, Nikki's company's forklift is likely to sit here unused, until somebody else leases the warehouse and takes it over as being his."

"I'm afraid you're right there. Nobody really cares."

"Sad. That company has been in the family for over a hundred years."

"What do you do when you don't have any family to take it over, and you can't sell it because you're too sick and too close to dying to care?"

"You do exactly what he did. You let it fade away into nothing."

It was sad when North could see what had once been a thriving, enterprising company.

They did a quick search on the forklifts and then walked toward Nikki.

"Did you find any information on this subleasing company, Booker & Sons?" Dan asked North.

"Nikki gave us some of the basics from the sublease. Name and phone number, contact information. Nothing unusual pops online. Our tech guys are investigating the head office out of the Ukraine. But I believe it was all handed over to you MI6 guys."

"Yes, the IT guys at the office are working on it," Dan said. "It's a holding company, which is to be expected, I guess."

North could see Nikki just sitting at the desk, pecking on the laptop. He poked his head in. "Anything?"

"Nothing much," she said. "Stan has been playing games here too. I don't think he's been around much. There's no paperwork. I checked the company email. There's nothing coming or going. Essentially it's been dead for weeks. They're just finishing up the last few orders. Hannah contacted all the clients, letting them know we were potentially shutting down and asking if they needed anything completed before then. I think, at that point, a lot of them jumped ship to other suppliers."

"Why would she do that? That's like a death knell for the company."

Nikki raised her head and smiled at him. "Hannah is one of those painfully honest people. She felt it would have been a huge disservice to all our customers if they couldn't continue to receive the products they normally do. She would at least give them as much notice as she could. At the same time, she was hoping they would sell the company, but, when there weren't any bites, and everyone went to other suppliers, there was really nothing left but to shut the doors."

"And it's just a couple desks anyway."

Nikki nodded. "And those are rented. The rental company will pick up the desks. The corporate office lease is over in all respects, so lock the doors as you walk out, and the same thing for the warehouse. It's done."

"Hannah needs to remember a forklift is here," North reminded her. "That's worth a few thousand pounds."

"True," Nikki said. "And it might be needed. I don't know."

"Just send her an email and ask. She might be able to sell it." He walked over to the other office to see Dan had it open already. "As long as it's you doing this," he said, "and not me."

Dan chuckled. "I'm acting under orders. It's all good."

The office was similar to the one he'd left Nikki in, with a single desk and chair, but this one had a file cabinet. He walked over and, using his handkerchief, pulled open one of the drawers. Inside were several files. "Don't know if this is of any interest." He riffled through them. There were various company names. He opened one folder that was particularly fat. "This is a chemical lab."

"Now *that* we need to know the name of."

"Why don't you just seize all this stuff? The men you saw who worked here are dead. We know the product was picked up here, and it was delivered to the other warehouse. You've seized that one. Why not this one?"

"We need to capture whoever killed those men, and the best place to find the next link is with this place. So we'll go through it, but we'll leave it open, and hopefully somebody will come along who we can pick up for questioning."

"Are you monitoring this warehouse then? Installing

cameras?"

"Techs will be in today," Dan said. "The desk isn't holding anything of any interest." He stood and walked over to the file cabinet. They checked the other drawers, which were empty. "Let me take a look at these. I'll photograph all the documents so we can do some research on any names we find." He checked his watch. "We should probably leave soon."

"Don't you want to wait until your techs arrive?"

"Yes, but not sure we need to be here. We could be under surveillance as it is."

They laid out the folders and snapped images, North working on one side and Dan on the other. North did all the small files with only one or two things in them and quickly replaced them as he went.

Dan was stuck on the big file, taking as many photographs as he could. Finally he closed it and said, "Did you get all the others?"

"Yeah, I did."

They stored away the big folder once more and closed the file drawer and stepped out of the office.

Nikki was waiting for them. "Are you done?" she asked. "I don't know why, but I'm starting to feel nervous."

North tucked her to him, dropped a kiss on her forehead before releasing her and said, "It should be all good."

With the second office door shut and locked behind them, she locked the other office door, and they stepped toward the front door. There, Dan hesitated.

North looked at him and said, "I know, right? We could always go out the back."

They made a sudden decision to lock the front door and slipped out the back.

Having already been in this location, North recognized where they were. The gloom was just settling in. "We'll slip around to the vehicle, but we'll take the long way."

She nodded. "I gather you were feeling the same nervousness I was."

"Oh, yeah," he said.

Dan stopped. "I'll wait here for you to get in the vehicle. If you see anybody out in front, let me know."

"Are we waiting for you?" Nikki asked.

Dan just smiled at her. "No, my team is on the way. We'll install some cameras, and, if we have somebody else coming in here right now, we'll pick him up for questioning."

She hesitated.

North looked at her and smiled. "We don't have any jurisdiction here, sweetie. He gets to say what we can and cannot do."

She glared at Dan. "You know it's not fair."

"All that product in there doesn't belong to your company," North explained to her. "We didn't even take a look to see what was in any of it."

Dan said, "I gave it a cursory look. Most of it was just crates and crates and crates. With codes and packing slips affixed, but it wasn't very obvious what was in it. I'm not leaving this place until it's been thoroughly checked over, and we have the cameras installed. Now you guys go home."

North nodded, wrapped his arm around Nikki's shoulders and tucked her up close. "Let's go." He turned back to Dan. "You got my number if you run into trouble in the next ten to fifteen minutes, before your team gets here. Call me."

Dan tilted his head in agreement. "I will."

Just as they headed around the next corner of the building, North heard the sound that made his stomach clench. There was a soft spit, followed by a second one. He didn't even bother turning to check on Dan. It was already too late.

He grabbed Nikki's hand and raced her across the street and up to the car. Without stopping, he tossed her inside, bolted into the driver's seat, turned on the engine, backed out of the parking lot and ripped around the block.

She stared at him in horror. "Please tell me that's not what I thought it was."

He gave her a grim look. "Unfortunately it was."

Chapter 11

S HE THOUGHT NORTH would drive her to her grand-dad's home, but he pulled over several blocks up ahead and called Jonas. "Dan has been hit. I'm pretty sure he's down and gone. We had already left the building. He was standing guard, waiting for the team to come. I was getting Nikki back to the vehicle. That's when we heard the spits."

"I'm on the way," Jonas said. "Where are you?"

"About six blocks away. I had to get her somewhere safe."

"Stay there. How did anybody know you were in there?"

"Same thing again. I'm sure they were watching the place. We were about to go out the front door, but I had a horrible feeling, as did Dan and Nikki, that maybe a welcome party was on the other side, so we locked the front and raced out the back. And honestly we were fine for at least five minutes while we reconvened, and then we took off. When we came around the second corner, we heard Dan go down."

"I hope you're wrong. But you did the right thing. I don't want Nikki involved any more than needed. Charles will never forgive me if something happens to her."

"I know, but you need a team here fast. That warehouse is full. All of the product in there supposedly belongs to that Booker & Son company, the subleasee. We took a lot of photographs from a chemical company folder we found, but honestly Dan had the bulk of those on his phone. I have a few, but that's it."

"When we hang up, start sending them my way. These men could easily have taken Dan's phone, and we'll have lost that information."

"Surrey Chemical Labs," North said suddenly. "The big fat folder Dan was taking pictures of was from a company called Surrey Chemical Labs."

"Okay. Let's hope his phone is still there when we arrive."

"What's your ETA?"

"Still about twelve minutes. But I've got two men approaching the scene in the next five minutes."

"Okay, call me back with an update." He sank back against the seat and rolled his head to look at Nikki.

She was staring at him, her eyes huge. She reached out a shaky hand.

He grasped it, half tugging her into his lap. "Easy," he whispered. "Just take it easy."

"But if they killed Dan ..." Her voice trembled. "He was a really nice man. He was just trying to help."

"In this business, really nice men die all the time." He brushed the strands of hair off her face. "And again we were in the wrong place at the wrong time."

"How did they know we'd be there?"

"I think they were waiting until somebody showed up. What we don't know is if they thought we worked for the company who imported those drugs or for the company that was leasing the warehouse. Remember how there's London Emporium, your company, and there's Booker & Sons, who leases warehouse space, but there is also Only the Best who ordered the wine. We don't know who or what is behind this. For all we know, we have a fourth party trying to exact revenge or to tie off loose ends. Your company is already done. Emporium will hardly be an issue."

"Maybe. But I really feel like we need to track down the other employees to make sure they are all okay. Especially Stan."

"We can do that. Maybe have Hannah call all the men to confirm, including the man who supposedly got a new job last week."

She nodded. "I can do that." As she went to sit back in the passenger seat again, she stopped, flung her arms around his neck and just hugged him tight. "I'm really scared right now."

He wrapped his arms around her, holding her close. "And with good reason. I won't sugarcoat the truth. We're in a very dangerous game at the moment. But remember. My priority is keeping you safe."

Nikki curled up in his arms. There was no space in the front seat to do this comfortably, but she didn't care one bit. He was holding her close, and, for the moment, that was enough. She hated to think Dan had been gunned down because of her. And she knew logically it wasn't because of her, but she still felt responsible. And it was terrible.

He leaned forward, kissed her on the forehead and whispered, "Sorry, sweetie. But I need you to sit back in your seat. I think we have company."

Instantly panic hit. She scrambled to her seat.

He tried to reassure her. "Sorry, that was the wrong thing to say. It's okay. I think it's Jonas arriving."

She sagged into her seat and peered between the two headrests behind them. When there was a rap on the window, she shrieked.

North reached over and grabbed her hand. "It's all right. It's okay."

She nodded mutely and sat in the corner, staring at Jonas, who peered through the window at her.

North lowered the window. "You surprised her," he said quietly.

The look on Jonas's face was filled with regret and sadness. "I'm sorry. It's been a tough day and a tough evening."

She nodded. "He is dead, isn't he?"

With a heavy sigh Jonas said, "Yes. I'm sorry."

"Me too." Tears collected in the corner of her eyes. "He didn't deserve that."

"None of us do," Jonas said. He looked over at North. "You didn't see anything?"

North shook his head. "No. Not only did we not see anything but we only heard the spits as we came around the second corner. Did you find his phone?"

"We did," Jonas said. "It was underneath him."

"Well, that's something. He got all the photos on the big file."

"We'll escort you back to Charles's place."

She leaned forward. "I can't have my grandfather in danger again."

At that Jonas chuckled. "His place is more like Fort Knox. The fact that Carl got the drop on him is already pissing your granddad off something awful."

She thought about it, remembering the office and the way he had such a high level of security to lock down the place, and she nodded. "Maybe that's for the best after all."

"It's definitely the best place to hole up in." He looked at North. "I've got two guys with me. One's going in the lead vehicle out front and one behind." He pointed to the one in front. "When he pulls out, you follow."

North nodded, closed the window and waited. When the lead car headed out, North pulled in behind it, and, sure enough, the one behind them tucked into place too.

She sighed. "Our government money at work again, I suppose."

"At least it's at work helping you this time," he said. "I've known governments to spend unbelievable amounts of money on the most foolish of things."

It was a slow but steady trip back to the townhome. When she got there, she waited until North exited the car, walked around and opened the door for her to get out. In every movement he made sure his body was between her and the rest of the world.

"I appreciate that you're trying to protect me," she whispered, "but I won't feel any better if you get hurt."

"If I get hurt, it's part of my job."

She almost missed her step at those words. They caused so much pain on the inside, and it was hard for her to even breathe. Is that what she was to him—a job?

Of course that's what she had started out being, but she'd hoped that, somewhere along the line, she'd become so much more. What a fool she was.

"What's the matter?" he asked, wrapping an arm around her, nudging her forward.

"Just your line about *it's the job*."

"It is," he stated matter-of-factly. "For a long time, over a decade, I've been putting my life at risk to help others."

"When is it time to stop doing that?"

"Maybe never," he said with a half smile. "Some of us are just natural-born guardians."

She thought about that and realized it was true. She had no right to be upset. He was doing what he was doing because he'd been asked to do it. "I guess I was hoping this was more than a job."

"It isn't *just* a job. Because I'm doing my job doesn't make it *just* a job." His voice was calm and low, but there was a powerful undercurrent to it.

She glanced up at him and gave him half a smile. "I'm glad."

He rested his hand on her lower back and nudged her forward again. "The sooner we're inside, the less chance we have of getting hit ourselves."

She gasped and almost raced to the door.

He chuckled, opened it and let her in. "I didn't mean to make you panic."

"No, but I was definitely dawdling." She turned to see her granddad walking toward her. She burst into tears and threw her arms around him. "Dan is dead."

He patted her on the shoulder and let her cry. She hated to be the weeping female, but it wasn't every day a good man was killed right behind you. When she calmed down, he motioned her into the sitting room. "You know what to do. Let's sit and have a cup of tea."

The mundaneness of it all made her give a hiccupping laugh. But, instead of sitting, she threw herself on the couch and stretched out. She was physically tired, but her emotional exhaustion wouldn't let her sleep to help her body recover.

North walked in, sat down and patted her on the knee. "With any luck it's all over."

"It won't be over until the sniper is killed or in prison."

"It would help to know who he is," Anders said as he walked in the room, crouching down beside her. "How are you?"

At his caring tone, hot tears filled the corners of her eyes again. "I'm fine." She sniffled. "I don't want to cry anymore. But it's just so hard. Dan was killed right behind us."

Anders nodded. "I heard the story. I'm so sorry." He straightened and looked at North. "Did you at least see anything inside the warehouse?"

"Except for the fact that it's completely full, no. We did take photos of most of the file cabinet contents, though there wasn't a lot. And, as long as Jonas has Dan's phone, then that's good, because he's the one who took all the photos of the large file we found on Surrey Chemical Labs."

"They could very well be the ones affiliated with this product, but we still need to find out who the sniper was and whether he's the only person we're looking for, or if he's just another hired hand. Also," Anders said, taking the seat on the opposite side of the coffee table, "we did full workups on Carl and Phillip. They've been in and out of jail for petty crimes, both of them, since high school."

"Well, that figures," North said. "Stunning examples of criminal types."

"At least from the slum side," Anders agreed. "We have a list of their known associates. Several have been questioned already, but so far nothing has shaken loose. Nobody ever wants to talk to the cops, and supposedly most people don't know what Carl has been up to for the last five years anyway. They said he's been pretty cheeky and downright mum about this job. They figured he got hooked into something really good, but he was staying quiet about it."

"Which is probably what kept him alive all this time," Nikki said. "Once you start talking, your life expectancy shortens."

"Exactly," Anders said. "We have a couple more names to contact. Two of his known associates were dead, four in prison."

"Wow. He keeps in good company, doesn't he?"

"Not so much. We're not expecting much more from the last two. But we have to run them down first, and that's not so easy. One might have left the country and gone to mainland Europe."

"I'm sure that's a problem, with people traveling back and forth all the time," North said. "And the last one?"

"There is some talk he might have been working at the same place. But then had a falling out. He disappeared about six months ago. His name is Scott."

"Nobody has heard from him since?"

Slowly Anders shook his head.

North sat back as if contemplating that news.

Nikki wondered what it meant, and then she realized. "So the smuggling boss killed him, right? Something went wrong, a falling out of thieves, whatever you want to call it, and that guy was taken out? That means they've taken out five people, that we know of, who worked with them—Scott, Carl, Phillip, plus Willy, the truck driver, and the receiving clerk at the second warehouse." She thought about that. "If it's a simple-enough operation, then the boss man doesn't need anybody else. He could have just been cleaning up."

"That's exactly what he's been doing," North said. "The question is whether he is done, and, if he is, what's he planning on doing next?"

"Running?" she hazarded a guess.

"Not likely," Anders said. "An awful lot of product remains here, and he has a full supply chain already established. All he needs is to stay underground, either steal

back or order more of these vials and get the distribution
going. There'll be some in that warehouse still, not to
mention whoever it is who's getting it will want more."

"And that puts us back to the company that these men
supposedly worked for."

"And funny enough, we can't find the person in charge.
Wilson Massey is the manager for the English division of
Booker & Sons. Making him a person of interest."

North studied her face. "Does the name mean anything
to you?"

She shook her head. "No, it doesn't. I've never heard it
before."

"Maybe call Hannah and ask her?"

Nikki sat up, pulled her phone from her pocket and dialed. "Hannah, do you know the manager for Booker &
Sons?"

"Not off the top of my head." Her voice sounded ex-
traordinarily tired. "And you should know Nathan took a
turn for the worse this afternoon. Looks like the end is much
sooner than we expected."

It was a blow after everything else she'd been through
today. "I'm so sorry. It's a terrible time for everyone right
now. I'm so sorry for you, Hannah. Obviously you have a
very close relationship with him."

"I do, and he will be sorely missed."

"Before I let you go, do you know the name Wilson
Massey?"

"Oh, that's who it is. That's the man we leased the
warehouse to."

"Did you do any reference checks or anything on him?"

"No, I doubt it. I think Nathan knew him from school.
So, when he needed some space, Nathan didn't have a

problem giving it to him. Is there a problem at the warehouse?"

"Yes, but the police are on it. They may contact you. I don't know." She didn't want to get into too many details. Hannah had enough going on with Nathan right now. And Nathan really didn't need to know on his deathbed how his friend might be smuggling in chemicals to distribute drugs in London and has been using his family's business to do this for years.

"As long as we no longer have product at the warehouse, it's not a big deal, is it?"

"I don't think it is. Stay strong, Hannah." As Nikki hung up, she looked at North and Anders. "Nathan took a turn for the worse this afternoon. Looks like the end is coming much faster. She recognized the name as the person who leased the warehouse space. Apparently he was an old friend of Nathan's from school."

"Right. So he just leased him the space and didn't realize it was being used for transporting illegal goods."

She shrugged. "We have no way to know. Product comes in. Product goes out. That's all we do. We bring it in, check it off the list, and we ship it back out again. According to Hannah, nothing left in the warehouse is ours anymore, but we should contact Stan and find out for sure. And you heard me ask her to check up on all four men. Stan isn't answering his phone."

"Right. But, if you give me his name, we'll get Jonas to check up on him."

She pulled up his name on her cell phone and handed it to Anders.

He entered it into his cell phone, then sent it off to Jonas. "Just to keep the chain of communication wide open," he explained. He looked at her intently. "You look like you could do with a nap."

"After she has some tea." Charles came in the doorway, pushing the cart in ahead of him.

She tried to sit up, but North gently pushed her back down again. Gratefully she collapsed. "I feel like bread that's been left on the counter too long," she said. "If you pick me up and put me down again too hard, I'll shatter."

"No shattering allowed," he said. "What you need is a bite to eat, a cup of tea, and then go to bed to grab a few hours."

"Considering I hardly got any sleep last night, that's probably not a bad idea," she said with half a smile. She shifted until she was reclining in the corner and accepted the cup of tea North held out for her. She took a sip and smiled at her grandfather. "As always, it's perfect."

"Like I've told you many a time," Charles said, "there is only one way to make perfect tea."

She chuckled. "It always turns out perfect for you but not so much for me."

He smiled. "You must learn to do it properly."

Privately she figured the problem was how she didn't have a whole lot that was proper about her. But her granddad exemplified the term. She smiled at him as he sat at the edge of his large Victorian chair and sipped his own tea. "Anything happen while we were gone?"

He shook his head. "It's all been quiet. Anders has been helping me fix the security. Once the power was cut, we had to do a bit of rerouting."

"So it wasn't all set to run off the other townhome?"

"Most of it was, not all of it. But it's all working again now."

She smiled. "Perfect." When her tea was done, she found herself falling asleep. She couldn't stop yawning. She stood up, wavered on her feet and said, "I think it's time for me to crash."

"Come on," North said. "I'll help you upstairs. You look like you won't make it as it is."

She let North wrap an arm around her shoulders, and together they walked to the bottom of the stairs. "Granddad, don't let me sleep too long. Just a couple hours."

"No problem," he said. "I'll wake you up soon."

She marched up the stairs with as much energy as she could find. At the top, she let out a heavy sigh. "It takes an effort to appear to be okay to everybody," she said with a half smile.

"It does, indeed." He motioned her down the hall to her bedroom.

She walked inside, sat down on the edge of her bed and crashed on top of the covers.

He reached for the blanket she kept folded at her feet, picked it up and tossed it over her. He leaned over and gave her a quick kiss on her cheek. "Now have a nap." And he walked out.

"Leave the door open," she cried out.

He froze at the doorway, turned to look back at her. "Of course I can do that."

He walked down the hall. She could hear his footsteps as he turned and headed to his room. It'd be good if he slept too. Neither of them had gotten much sleep last night. She could feel sleep tugging at her, and gratefully she slid into its welcoming embrace.

NORTH OPENED THE bedroom door, checked that everything was okay in his room, walked across to Anders's room and checked it out as well. Inside, his instincts said something was off, but he couldn't place it. He hadn't done a quick search of Nikki's room while he was in there, beyond a cursory glance. But now he found himself wishing he had done a full-on search. He pulled out his phone and texted Anders. **Something is off.**

Unable to help himself, North went door to door, ensuring nobody was upstairs and that nothing appeared out of order. Finally he was back at her room. With the big double doors still open, he could see her sleeping on the bed. She appeared to be fine, and everything in her room seemed normal. But something was not normal. He just couldn't figure out what it was.

He slid to stand against the wall and listened in on her room. But he couldn't hear anything. Just then Anders started up the stairs. He stopped when he saw North leaning against the wall. North held a finger to his lips.

With a frown, Anders slipped off his shoes, climbed up the railing and landed beside him gently.

North whispered, "Something is wrong. I want to search her room."

Anders nodded. They both swept through the room at the same time, silent and deadly, one going down and to the left, the other one going upright and to the right. North was on the left. He headed for the bathroom, gave it a full check but found nothing in there. Already Anders was checking under the bed and found nothing there.

Nikki slept on.

That left the big double-doored closet, which he suspected had a huge walk-in section. Definitely big enough for someone to hide in. But the doors were closed, and he wasn't sure he could open them without waking her up.

Anders scooted under the bed and came up on the other side. With one guy on either side of the closet doors, they each reached for one of the doors, pulled them open.

The intruder burst forth.

He reached for North, who tumbled back slightly at the sudden impact, and Anders jumped on the intruder's back from behind. The guy struggled to get his weapon lined up to hit North. Anders grabbed his gun arm and tried to knock it away from him. Suddenly free, North crouched, spun and gave a dropkick, then clocked the man in the jaw, sending him flying backward.

Lopsided, with Anders still on the guy's back, he tumbled backward, hitting the floor, rolling. North was on him in an instant. The fight was hard and heavy, and nowhere near as fast as he would have liked it. The intruder fought back with deadly military precision. Finally, with a hard right uppercut to the same spot that he'd kicked, North took him out with one last blow. The intruder flopped to the ground, unconscious. Straddling him, North sat on top of the man's legs to catch his breath.

Anders dropped down beside him. "Who do you think it is?"

"Pull the balaclava off his head, and let's find out," he said.

"Are you done yet?" came Nikki's exasperated voice from the bed.

He turned in surprise to see Nikki sitting up, the blanket he'd tossed over her clutched to her chest as she stared at them.

"I couldn't believe it. Once Anders went under my bed,

I almost had a heart attack. And then I realized you thought somebody was in the closet." She hopped off the bed, wrapped the blanket around her shoulders and walked over to look at the man on the floor. "Take that mask off him. I'd like to see who this is."

They pulled it off to see a middle-aged man, maybe in his late forties.

She stared at him in shock. "That's Stan, our warehouse manager."

"I think he's also our smuggler ... maybe even the sniper." Anders held up the handgun with a silencer at the end of it. "I'd bet all odds this is the gun used to kill Dan too."

Her gaze went from Anders to North and then back down to Stan. "I don't understand," she said. "Why would he do that?"

"It'll take a little bit to bring him around," North said. "But I suggest we ask him ourselves. Once we've got all the answers, then we'll call Jonas."

She laughed. "Well, you might want to do it that way. I'm not so sure my granddad will agree."

"Oh, I don't know," North said. "I think he bends the rules just fine whenever he wants to."

She reached down and kissed him impulsively. "How did you possibly know Stan was in here?"

North stood so he was beside her, holding her in his arms. "I was heading down the hallway, when something told me not to leave. That something was off. I checked my room and Anders's room, and then I sent him a text warning. I went through every bedroom and realized that really the only place that was an issue was your room."

She glanced at Anders. "So you came to join him?"

"Of course. We're a team," he said.

She smiled and then looked at Stan. The smile fell off her face. "I can't believe it. I wonder if Scottie, Stan's assistant, knows about this?"

"Well, there's a Scott who used to hang around Carl all the time. He hasn't been seen in months."

She frowned. "Surely it's not the same Scottie," she said slowly, "but I can't remember when I saw him last."

"How long ago were you at the warehouse before last week?"

She shook her head. "I can't be sure without my calendar, but I don't think I've been at the warehouse for a good six maybe seven weeks, and, even if I was there, it doesn't mean Scottie was too. There's a good chance I haven't seen Scottie in two or three months or more," she admitted. "For all I know, he quit his job too."

The two men looked at each other and down at Stan. "He could have been running a side racket for a long time. Using the facility, keeping track of your business and working together with Booker & Sons. It makes a whole lot of sense if nobody else but him handles the physical shipments. He was here on the spot and worked alone. He could have brought in anything he wanted and shipped it out all on his own. You guys wouldn't even have seen the paperwork unless he wanted you to. Somehow this last shipment was screwed up, and he let the paperwork slip."

She stared at them aghast. "So you think Stan's been using Emporium to run illegal goods through? I sure hope none of this comes back on us."

"Maybe it's a good thing Nathan might pass away before he finds out what's happened to the family company he cherished," North said. "Because something like this, well, it'd be enough of a shock that it could kill him outright."

North stayed close to Nikki. As the day wore on, she looked more and more exhausted, more upset. She had called Hannah, given her a quick explanation of what had been going on. Hannah's upset had been only compounded by Nathan's continued poor condition. At this point, they doubted Nathan would regain consciousness. And somehow his company had to be shut down and cleared of all wrongdoing. And that would be a little harder to do now that they had learned of Stan's involvement.

"Do you remember what happened to Scottie?"

"No," Hannah said between her sobs. "Stan said he fired him. We stopped his paychecks, and I never heard any more."

"Did he give a reason why he fired him?"

"Said he was incompetent. That's all I know," she said, sniffling heavily. "I can't believe all this is going on. We were almost done. In another week, the company would be closed."

"Essentially it is closed. It could have been closed several weeks ago."

"Sure, but Nathan wanted to keep it open so any customers could reach us for as long as they needed to. Whether for information like referrals, files, records, things like that. We haven't taken any new orders in a while."

"Well, the warehouse is quite full," Nikki said. "We'll have to sort through what Stan might have had a hand in. But you need to understand MI6 is involved."

"Why are they involved?" Hannah's voice was so full of surprise that she shrieked out the words. "This isn't about terrorism."

"It depends what they find is in those vials," Nikki said. "I understand it's a component of a drug used in street drugs."

"This is just awful, just awful," Hannah cried out.

"I'm so sorry to tell you all this. I just found out myself when I was there on Thursday. A couple men threatened me in the warehouse. Stan wasn't there, and I didn't know what to do. I came to my grandfather's place to calm down, but the two warehouse guys came here and attacked him, and then they came back in and tried to attack me."

Nikki knew it was too much for Hannah. Hannah's whole focus was on Nathan's health. And what she had thought was an ending of one man's passion had become something others had abused. "I'll let you go. Again I'm so sorry."

"It's not your fault," Hannah said in a worried tone. "But it's a really difficult ending. I thought for sure we would just close the last door, and we'd be done."

"Well, essentially that's what's happened. But MI6 is now going through the warehouse. I don't exactly understand what and how, but, because there have been several murders of the smuggling crew, plus MI6 had some agents killed too, they'll go through everything with a fine-tooth comb." Nikki hesitated, then added, "I gave them your contact information."

"Yes, yes, of course. It doesn't matter. The office will be closed in a week. I have all the files. Almost everything is digitized by now. I'll file it all, pay the last of the taxes, and it's a done deal."

"I guess if we knew what we were coming to, we should have closed the business on the last day of the year. Just to make taxes easier."

"Nathan and I had talked about that," she said sadly. "But he was much more optimistic about his future. He thought for sure he'd have another couple years."

Nikki didn't say anything, but, of course, that was just one of the sad things about disease. It didn't march to anybody else's tune but its own. Finally she said goodbye and hung up the phone and sat there.

Dinner was long over. The men were sitting with a whiskey, still hashing out the events of the day. The MI6 men had left before the meal was prepped. North and Anders hadn't been allowed to ask any questions, and that had been upsetting in itself.

"We should have kept the MI6 men here."

"You know we couldn't do that." Her grandfather's tone was as firm as it had been any other time.

When they had taken Stan to Charles, he'd phoned Jonas. Jonas had shown up and whisked Stan away. As much as she really wanted answers, she knew she'd get some eventually, but she didn't wish Stan an easy time with Jonas. Jonas had lost four of his men and one, Dan, had been a good friend apparently. And, if Stan had anything to do with that, well, he wouldn't find his future very friendly.

"Besides," North said, "there really weren't too many questions to ask."

"The one I really wanted to know was whether that was the end of the men," she said quietly. "Or did Stan have a partner who even now is skulking around the outside of the house. Who is the boss here?"

"Jonas has been watching the warehouse as well as this place since we got called here. Jonas had already done a full sweep of this area right after we caught Stan. Remember that Anders went out to take a look too."

"So then my question really is, is somebody still inside the house?" she said. "I'm not certain I'll sleep tonight."

North reached over and patted her hand. "You'll be fine."

She shook her head. "I'm not so sure about that." She glanced at her grandfather. "Please tell me that you've searched the other townhome."

He looked at her steadily. "Why would I need to?"

She raised both hands in frustration. "Fine. I'm just a worrywart. I know that. But that was a little bit too close for comfort, to wake up and find you guys tackling that man in my room." She put down her teacup and stood. "I'll go have a bath and go to bed. Good night, everyone." And she headed to the stairs.

Chapter 12

IT TOOK EVERY ounce of her courage to climb that stairway alone. At the top, Nikki stopped, took several deep breaths and quietly approached her bedroom. She hadn't been back here since they had found Stan. There were just ever-so-slight differences, the evidence of violence. Like the closet doors remained open—where Stan had been hiding—and the small throw rug inside had been scrunched to the side.

The bedroom carpet had been brushed up, where the men had fought outside the closet, and her bed had been nudged slightly to the side. She walked over, gently smoothed the carpet with her feet, put the bed back into place, stepped into the closet with the lights on and ran her hands over the hangers, making sure nobody else was inside. Reassured the place was empty, she headed into the bathroom and brushed her teeth. She was thinking about a bath but wasn't sure she had enough energy.

Maybe just a shower. She walked back into the bedroom, laid her camisole and shorts on the bed, closed and locked the doors to her bedroom, quickly stripped down to her underwear and walked back into the bathroom to turn on the hot water.

She opened the glass door as a hand came up and slapped across her mouth. She tried to struggle, but he was too strong, too big, and, from the look in his eyes, too pissed off to allow her to do anything. Realizing resistance was futile, she sagged in his arms and waited for whatever came next. Mentally she kept screaming for North.

If his intuition had been so strong earlier, why the hell wasn't he here with her now?

The bathroom door opened as the intruder pushed her, his arm still wrapped around her throat, his hand still slapped over her mouth, and he said, "I want you to lie down on the bed. If you scream, I'll snap your neck like the twig it is. Do you understand?"

She nodded. His tone was dead, almost lifeless.

But there was a heavy French accent to it. She didn't know who he was, but she had no doubt he would be completely fine carrying out all he said. He let go of her, and she raced to the bed and pulled her T-shirt over her head.

He snorted. "I have no desires for you physically. You couldn't be less my type."

She sat with the covers pulled up to her chest, trembling. She was desperately thinking of how to alert North just one floor below. Why the hell had she locked her doors? Of course she'd been trying to keep the world at bay, but instead all she'd done was locked the world inside.

"Where did they take Stan?" he asked.

Knowing there was no point in lying, she said, "Some men from the government came and took him away."

"Why the government?"

"Five of the men you killed worked for them."

His gaze turned dark. "Yes, the four outside this home. ... And the man outside the warehouse."

She hesitated and then nodded. "Dan was a good man," she snapped. "You didn't have to kill him."

"I didn't kill him. It was Stan."

"Why don't you just take your drugs and leave," she snapped.

His gaze, which had been searching her room, zeroed in on her face. "What do you know about the drugs?"

She shrugged. "I know they were hidden under the cases of wine."

"Well then, you obviously know too much," he said, his voice silky smooth.

And she froze. *Shit, shit, shit.* Her and her big mouth. "That's what the men said. I don't know anything about it," she said hurriedly.

He sneered. "You might as well keep talking."

"I don't know anything," she said. "Why don't you tell me something? You intend to snap my neck anyway."

"That's just a trick to get me to talk."

"So what?" she said. "You can't be afraid of me."

He waved a hand at her as if she was a gnat irritating him. "Of course I'm not afraid of you. What's to be afraid of? You don't weigh more than eight stones."

Interesting. Despite his French accent, he's using a British measurement. ... What the hell did France use for its measurements anyway?

"Besides you're a nobody."

"And you're a somebody?" She shifted ever-so-slightly closer to the night table. One of her long nail files was on top of it.

"I am in my group, yes. But, if I don't take care of this mess, you can bet I'll be a nobody just as fast." He swore softly. "This is ridiculous. How the hell did all this go to shit?"

"I don't know," she said, her adrenaline gone, leaving

her suddenly weary. She shifted, propping the pillow behind her, grabbing the nail file and tucking it underneath the pillow as she settled back. "This has all been a nightmare."

"It was Stan, wasn't it?" he snapped. "He is the one who screwed up."

"I don't know," she said. "Maybe he let us see paperwork we shouldn't have. But it was the double order that made no sense."

"A stupid clerical error. Brought down by something so simple."

"You're Massey? The manager of Booker & Sons?" She knew she shouldn't ask anything, but it was so hard not to want to know what was going on.

He shot her a hard look. "And the owner of Only the Best—which will now cease to exist. But it was the best way to move the products and have no one know. That network has been functioning for two years. It was too much to lose. I wondered if Stan was setting up his own distribution channel. But I'm unlikely to know the truth at this point. I trusted him and didn't want to think the worst of him. Stan has always been a great asset."

"As he screwed the company he was working for, I imagine he was trying to screw you too. But you can't ask him because the government has him. So you're the boss? The one who ordered someone to run our vehicle off the road? Had your men break into Granddad's house? Had Stan take out the government men and your own men? How could you do that?"

He nodded again. "Whatever. I have to get the hell out of here."

"How the hell did you get in anyway?"

"I came in when you were all fussing over Carl. I let Stan

in much later." He gave her a wry smile. "I have to admit I didn't jump out and help him because he was a perfect patsy."

"Where the hell were you hiding?"

"I was still in the closet," he said. "There were two of us in there, but Stan wanted to jump out first, so I let him. Everybody caught him and disappeared." He tilted his head back and groaned. "But, for Stan to take the fall, I need to disappear. Start again in France. Set up a new network after enough time has gone by. Reconnect with the buyers ..."

She could imagine how it had all happened because she'd been here. It had been a surprise, and they'd been so concerned with Stan. Once they'd realized who he was, a quick glance in the closet would have been all they'd done. "Can you go out the window?" she asked hopefully. She motioned at the big windows beside her. "There's a fire escape in the back bedroom."

"I know. That's how Stan and I got in." He looked at her with sudden interest. "Why are you trying to help me?"

She snorted. "I want to get out of this alive."

"And you just might." He walked over to the bedroom doors, thinking.

"Please just go and leave me alone."

He turned to look at her. "I wish I could." He pulled out a handgun, the same kind as Stan had had, with a silencer on the end.

She started screaming as she threw herself to the floor and scooted under the bed. In the background she heard a hard spit. Then another as Massey approached her bed.

The bedroom doors burst open just then, and she watched as North flung Massey to his back and then beat Massey's face with his fists.

Anders struggled to pull North off the guy. "Hey, easy, easy. We need him alive."

Finally North sat back on his knees, catching his breath as he glared at the man on the floor. "Why the hell do we have to keep him alive? Pieces of shit like this don't deserve to live."

Anders shoved North off the guy and said, "Go take care of Nikki." Anders checked Massey on the floor. "He's still breathing." He pulled out his phone, and, while she watched, he called Jonas again.

North dropped to the floor next to the bed beside her. "Come on out."

She struggled out from under her bed, took one look at his face, threw her arms around him and just hung on tight.

"I shouldn't have let you come up the stairs alone," he snapped, crushing her against his chest. "As soon as you left, I knew it was wrong. By the time you hit the top of the stairs, I was already coming this way. But I got to the door, and I thought I heard you in the bathroom, so I hesitated. Then I heard a male voice. And I knew you were in trouble."

"I locked my doors," she said with a head shake. "I just wanted the world to go away for a few minutes."

He pushed her head against his chest and held her tight. "It's done. It'll be just fine."

She stood trembling in his arms. "Are you sure?"

He leaned back and smiled at her, tilted her face up and kissed her long and hard. "Yes, I'm sure."

She stared at him in wonder. Her attention was caught by Anders, who picked up the unconscious man and flung him over his shoulder. He stopped at the doorway and turned. "You guys have about forty-five minutes to get your shit together. Then Jonas will be here." And he turned and shut the door behind him.

They could hear him stomp across the hallway, heading toward the stairwell.

She looked at North and smiled. "What did he mean by that?"

North shrugged self-consciously. "I don't know."

She peered up into his gaze. "You care, right?"

His face turned red.

She nodded. "I care too."

He stared at her steadily. "Yeah? But how much?"

Uncomfortable again, she shrugged, unconsciously mimicking his shoulder movement. "Enough to consider moving to the US," she announced.

His gaze lit up. "We could travel back and forth and see your granddad all the time."

"And, if you ever do any jobs over here, I could come back for a visit."

"I don't know if you would consider Texas as a place to relocate."

"I don't care where I go. I was looking for a reason, and I think maybe I found it."

He tucked her into his arms, lowered his head and kissed her.

She leaned back, looked up at him and smiled. "So do you think Anders meant that we have that much time?"

"We definitely have time," he said. "But I don't want to waste what we have by trying to rush it."

She snickered. "I'm barely wearing anything. At the speed we're going, I suspect we'll have time for a quickie and a shower before Jonas gets here."

"Will you be embarrassed if you go downstairs afterward to meet all those men, when, from our wet hair and change of clothes, they'll know what we were doing?"

She gave him a flat stare. "Hell no. You're mine, and I'm yours. As soon as they realize that, the better for all of us." And this time she slid her arms up his chest, around his neck and through the curls in his hair. She pulled his head down. "So let's just make it fast for our first time."

As his lips crushed down on hers, she smiled and pressed her body flat against him from chest to hips. "Now that's more like it," she whispered against his lips, nipping at his bottom lip, then letting her tongue stroke across it. The only reason he let her go now was so he could strip down.

And strip he did. In two seconds flat the man standing before her, proud and erect, was completely nude. She tossed her T-shirt over her head, reached behind, unhooked her bra and stepped out of her panties. Enjoying the beautiful sight before her, she stroked his chest, his shoulders, his massive biceps. "You are incredibly fit," she said in wonder.

"It's part of the work I do," he admitted. "I spend a lot of time staying in this shape."

"And I'm glad for it. It saved my sorry ass more than a few times already."

He stepped forward, reached around and gently stroked her curvy back. "As asses go, my dear, this one is perfect. I have no intention of letting anybody hurt it." He picked her up and, in a quick move, tossed her on the bed.

She shrieked with laughter as she quickly realigned on the bed and opened her thighs, making room for him as he came down on top of her. "Make me forget what just happened," she whispered. "Please."

He crushed his lips against hers, with his hands, his body, teasing, exploring as his mouth moved from her lips to her chin to her throat, thereafter finding first one breast and then the other, and the valley in between. His hands stroking, caressing, gently sliding down, not missing a single inch of her bare body. When he stroked the inside of her thighs, between the curls at the apex, she moaned, her hips rising. He slid a finger inside, gently wiggling it deeper and deeper. She twisted her thighs, opening them wider and wider. With his thumb he gently massaged the tiny button in the hidden folds of her skin until she was gasping and clutching the bedding as her body arched in joy.

"Please," she whispered. "Please do it now."

But he was insistent on slowing the pace a bit. He let his fingers slowly pull out and then slide back in again, stroking, pressing, teasing her. As her body wept for joy, he lowered his head and took her right breast deep into his mouth, suckling the nipple like a babe. She cried out, her body twisting, her hands pulling at his head, trying to tuck him up closer. Her body had already warmed and softened, waiting for him, dying for his possession. She needed him inside her to complete this union she had known, right from the beginning, had to be. She'd never met anyone quite so dynamic, anybody so essentially perfect for her from the first moment on.

It had been days of stress and nightmarish events, so she hadn't had a chance to clue in on a more intimate level about who and what this man would be for her. But she knew now. And she had no intention of holding back. She pulled him over her, whispering, "I don't want to come without you."

He lifted his head, his fingers sliding free to gently cover the other nipple in her own juices before he turned and latched on tight. Her hips lifted as he rearranged, shifting to settle in deeper between them. While his lower body rested at the heart of her, he suckled her breast hard and deep, lightly nipping at the tip.

She groaned and moaned, and then she demanded, "Now."

And he plunged deep, his body stilling as he was centered right at her core. She cried out, a slight whimper that became a full-born climax when it rippled through her. But he wouldn't let her stop there. He started to move, withdrawing and entering faster and faster, deeper, stronger, then shifting their positions, rocking her body as he took complete and total possession of every bit of her.

Finally she could feel him clenching hard above her, a deep guttural groan rising from his chest, pouring out of his throat. She reached up, clutched him hard and raised herself to meet him with several hip thrusts, feeling a second climax rolling through her.

He dropped beside her, tucking her to him, pulling her close against his heart. Wrapped in each other's arms, she lay trembling against his chest, loving the sound of his heart pounding under her ear.

"Do we have to go back downstairs?" she whispered.

He clutched her to him and held her tight. "You know something? Maybe we don't."

"Will they care?"

Laughter rumbled up his chest. "I don't. Do you?"

She lifted her head and smiled at him. "Hell no. I suggest we stay here for the rest of the night. We'll face the music in the morning."

He stroked her cheeks and forehead and said, "No music. Just joy. Anders already knew, and so did your grandfather."

Tears came to her eyes as she whispered, "I'll still have trouble leaving him."

"I know," he said. "If you're not ready yet …"

She placed a finger across his lips. "I can't come right now anyway because I have to finish this job with Emporium. I have to take care of my flat. And I need some time with my grandfather."

He nodded. "I can stay for a couple days right now. But then I'll have to return to the States or head out to another job. I'll be traveling a lot."

She smiled. "That's okay. I'm not exactly sure what I'll do, but I'll find something."

He pulled her down. "Really what I found is you. And that makes everything about this trip worthwhile." He kissed her again.

She slid her hands around his neck and played with the curls at the back of his nape. When she could, she pulled herself away a little bit so she could look at him. "You sure it's not too fast?"

He gave her a wicked grin. "Sweetie, in my world, this is totally normal."

She stared into his gaze, gauging his seriousness, but what she could read made her heart thump away in joy. "So you're sure?"

"Are you?" he asked.

She nodded. "You're my hero. I'm never letting you go."

This time she lowered her head to his and kissed him. A kiss of today and the kiss of tomorrow. And, if they were lucky, a kiss for forever.

And she'd never been happier.

Epilogue

ANDERS RENAU SAT downstairs with Charles, celebrating, holding cut-crystal glasses of whiskey. Anders smiled and said, "Another one bites the dust."

Charles chuckled. "Good timing. I was really starting to worry she'd never find anybody."

"And I thought we were talking about the assignment." Anders put down his whiskey glass, pulled out his phone and sent Levi a quick message, letting him know about the change in relationship status for North.

The response was almost instantaneous. **Interesting. And not unexpected. The unknown was which one of you two she would choose.**

He read the message to Charles.

Charles nodded. "Levi and I had already discussed that. But we figured she'd make a choice in her own time." He studied Anders. "You're not upset, I hope?"

Anders grinned. "Hell no. She was not meant to be for me. She and North are perfect together."

"That's what I think too," Charles added.

Levi sent another message. **You've got two more days there, if you choose to spend them in England. Then you have a job in Switzerland.**

"Oh, good. I'll be in Switzerland after this," Anders said. "I wonder if North is supposed to travel with me."

"Maybe," Charles said. "Nikki won't leave England just

yet. She has to finish her job here, and I'm sure she'll want to stick around and see that the business shuts down properly. So she'll be detained at least for another week."

Anders sent a message back to Levi. **Switzerland sounds great. What about North?**

He can stay in England for a couple more days if he wants.

Laughing out loud, Anders hit Reply. **I guarantee you that he'll want to spend those days here.** He considered this new assignment for a moment. "I wonder why Switzerland? I haven't heard any chatter concerning that country."

"That's one country I haven't been to for a long time. It's beautiful," Charles said. "I've spent a lot of time in Geneva and Lausanne. And, of course, Zermatt for the standard tourist trip."

Anders nodded thoughtfully. "I've been skiing at several locations in Switzerland, but I've never been there strictly for business."

"It sounds like it will be work this time."

His phone buzzed again. It was Levi. **You'll be meeting Dezi and Reyes Handleman en route too.**

What's the job?

Retrieving a package. An expensive package.

Alive or dead?

But instead of texting a reply, Levi called. When Anders answered, Levi said, laughing, "She is alive and well and kicking mad."

"Who is she, and why are we retrieving her?"

"She is a specialist in glaciers. Don't ask me for more details because I really don't know anything more. But she is one of those specialists who measures the ice melt and the damage done in the retreat of icebergs."

"And we're retrieving her why?"

"Her father is a senator. He's in trouble and has received threats, putting his daughter in danger too. If you don't want to go to Switzerland, just say so."

"I'm delighted to go to Switzerland. And I don't mind picking up this package," he said. "The feistier, the better."

"Oh, you'll love this job then. I'll text you her name when I get off." And Levi hung up on him.

Anders grabbed the whiskey, held it up to Charles and said, "To my next job in Switzerland."

The men clinked glasses together and settled back to enjoy the fire. Anders couldn't help but think this job was something he was actually looking forward to. He adored women. And, like he had told Levi, *the feistier, the better.* She might not want to return with him, but she really wouldn't get much of a choice.

His phone buzzed. He looked at the name of the woman he was collecting and laughed. **Angelica**. ... Perfect, chances were good she wouldn't want anything to do with Anders.

Too bad. She would come with him—whether she wanted to or not.

This concludes Book 15 of Heroes for Hire: North's Nikki.

Read about Anders's Angel: Heroes for Hire, Book 16

Heroes for Hire: Anders's Angel (Book #16)

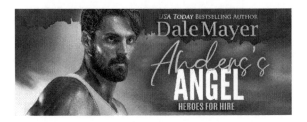

Anders Renau is sent to Switzerland by his employer, Legendary Securities, to retrieve a glaciologist. Her father faces a political nightmare that's made him worried enough to hire a former Navy SEAL to make sure his daughter isn't used as leverage against him.

An expert in an otherwise male-dominated field, Angela Ainsworth has spent her life studying snow and ice in order to cope with the never-ending heartaches associated with her parents' divorce and her own fiancé's betrayal. When Anders come barreling into her life, ordering her to return home on her father's orders, she's far from impressed...and she has absolutely no intention of obeying.

Anders loves Switzerland but, given the circumstances, he'd rather be anywhere else besides here, where this stubborn beauty wants nothing to do with him or her father's political agenda she'd tried to escape long ago. Despite her attitude, and regardless of the instant attraction that flares between them, Anders has to keep Angela safe in a world more hostile than any he's ever encountered before.

Book 16 is available now!
To find out more visit Dale Mayer's website.
http://smarturl.it/andersDM

Other Military Series by Dale Mayer

SEALs of Honor
Heroes for Hire
SEALs of Steel
The K9 Files
The Mavericks
Bullards Battle
Hathaway House
Terkel's Team

Ryland's Reach: Bullard's Battle (Book #1)

Welcome to a new stand-alone but interconnected series from Dale Mayer. This is Bullard's story—and that of his team's. All raw, rough, incredibly capable men who have one goal: to find out who was behind the attack on their leader, before the attacker, or attackers, return to finish the job.

Stay tuned for more nonstop action as the men narrow down their suspects … and find a way to let love back into their own empty lives.

His rescue from the ocean after a horrible plane explosion was his top priority, in any way, shape, or form. A small sailboat and a nurse to do the job was more than Ryland hoped for.

When Tabi somehow drags him and his buddy Garret onboard and surprisingly gets them to a naval ship close by, Ryland figures he'd used up all his luck and his friend's too. Sure enough, those who attacked the plane they were in weren't content to let him slowly die in the ocean. No. Surviving had made him a target all over again.

Tabi isn't expecting her sailing holiday to include the rescue of two badly injured men and then to end with the loss of her beloved sailboat. Her instincts save them, but now she finds it tough to let them go—even as more of Bullard's team members come to them—until it becomes apparent that not only are Bullard and his men still targets ... but she is too.

B ULLARD CHECKED THAT the helicopter was loaded with their bags and that his men were ready to leave.

He walked back one more time, his gaze on Ice. She'd never looked happier, never looked more perfect. His heart ached, but he knew she remained a caring friend and always would be. He opened his arms; she ran into them, and he held her close, whispering, "The offer still stands."

She leaned back and smiled up at him. "Maybe if and when Levi's been gone for a long enough time for me to forget," she said in all seriousness.

"That's not happening. You two, now three, will live long and happy lives together," he said, smiling down at the woman knew to be the most beautiful, inside and out. She would never be his, but he always kept a little corner of his heart open and available, in case she wanted to surprise him and to slide inside.

And then he realized she'd already been a part of his heart all this time. That was a good ten to fifteen years by now. But she kept herself in the friend category, and he understood because she and Levi, partners and now parents, were perfect together.

Bullard reached out and shook Levi's hand. "It was a hell of a blast," he said. "When you guys do a big splash, you really do a *big* splash."

Ice laughed. "A few days at home sounds perfect for me now."

"It looks great," he said, his hands on his hips as he surveyed the people in the massive pool surrounded by the palm trees, all designed and decked out by Ice. Right beside all the war machines that he heartily approved of. He grinned at her. "When are you coming over to visit?" His gaze went to Levi, raising his eyebrows back at her. "You guys should come over for a week or two or three."

"It's not a bad idea," Levi said. "We could use a long holiday, just not yet."

"That sounds familiar." Bullard grinned. "Anyway, I'm off. We'll hit the airport and then pick up the plane and head home." He added, "As always, call if you need me."

Everybody raised a hand as he returned to the helicopter and his buddy who was flying him to the airport. Ice had volunteered to shuttle him there, but he hadn't wanted to take her away from her family or to prolong the goodbye. He hopped inside, waving at everybody as the helicopter lifted. Two of his men, Ryland and Garret, were in the back seats. They always traveled with him.

Bullard would pick up the rest of his men in Australia. He stared down at the compound as he flew overhead. He preferred his compound at home, but damn they'd done a nice job here.

With everybody on the ground screaming goodbye, Bullard sailed over Houston, heading toward the airport. His two men never said a word. They all knew how he felt about Ice. But not one of them would cross that line and say anything. At least not if they expected to still have jobs.

It was one thing to fall in love with another man's woman, but another thing to fall in love with a woman who was so unique, so different, and so absolutely perfect that you knew, just knew, there was no hope of finding anybody else like her. But she and Levi had been together way before Bullard had ever met her, which made it that much more heartbreaking.

Still, he'd turned and looked forward. He had a full roster of jobs himself to focus on when he got home. Part of him was tired of the life; another part of him couldn't wait to head out on the next adventure. He managed to run everything from his command centers in one or two of his locations. He'd spent a lot of time and effort at the second one and kept a full team at both locations, yet preferred to spend most of his time at the old one. It felt more like home to him, and he'd like to be there now, but still had many more days before that could happen.

The helicopter lowered to the tarmac, he stepped out, said his goodbyes and walked across to where his private plane waited. It was one of the things that he loved, being a pilot of both helicopters and airplanes, and owning both birds himself.

That again was another way he and Ice were part of the same team, of the same mind-set. He'd been looking for another woman like Ice for himself, but no such luck. Sure, lots were around for short-term relationships, but most of them couldn't handle his lifestyle or the violence of the world that he lived in. He understood that.

The ones who did had a hard edge to them that he found difficult to live with. Bullard appreciated everybody's being alert and aware, but if there wasn't some softness in the women, they seemed to turn cold all the way through.

As he boarded his small plane, Ryland and Garret following behind, Bullard called out in his loud voice, "Let's go, slow pokes. We've got a long flight ahead of us."

The men grinned, confident Bullard was teasing, as was his usual routine during their off-hours.

"Well, we're ready, not sure about you though …" Ryland said, smirking.

"We're waiting on you this time," Garret added with a chuckle. "Good thing you're the boss."

Bullard grinned at his two right-hand men. "Isn't that the truth?" He dropped his bags at one of the guys' feet and said, "Stow all this stuff, will you? I want to get our flight path cleared and get the hell out of here."

They'd all enjoyed the break. He tried to get over once a year to visit Ice and Levi and same in reverse. But it was time to get back to business. He started up the engines, got confirmation from the tower. They were heading to Australia for this next job. He really wanted to go straight back to Africa, but it would be a while yet. They'd refuel in Honolulu.

Ryland came in and sat down in the copilot's spot, buckled in, then asked, "You ready?"

Bullard laughed. "When have you ever known me *not* to be ready?" At that, he taxied down the runway. Before long he was up in the air, at cruising level, and heading to Hawaii. "Gotta love these views from up here," Bullard said. "This place is magical."

"It is once you get up above all the smog," he said. "Why Australia again?"

"Remember how we were supposed to check out that newest compound in Australia that I've had my eye on? Besides the alpha team is coming off that ugly job in Sydney. We'll give them a day or two of R&R then head home."

"Right. We could have some equally ugly payback on that job."

Bullard shrugged. "That goes for most of our jobs. It's the life."

"And don't you have enough compounds to look after?"

"Yes I do, but that kid in me still looks to take over the world. Just remember that."

"Better you go home to Africa and look after your first two compounds," Ryland said.

"Maybe," Bullard admitted. "But it seems hard to not continue expanding."

"You need a partner," Ryland said abruptly. "That might ease the savage beast inside. Keep you home more."

"Well, the only one I like," he said, "is married to my best friend."

"I'm sorry about that," Ryland said quietly. "What a shit deal."

"No," Bullard said. "I came on the scene last. They were always meant to be together. Especially now they are a family."

"If you say so," Ryland said.

Bullard nodded. "Damn right, I say so."

And that set the tone for the next many hours. They landed in Hawaii, and while they fueled up everybody got off to stretch their legs by walking around outside a bit as this was a small private airstrip, not exactly full of hangars and tourists. Then they hopped back on board again for takeoff.

"I can fly," Ryland offered as they took off.

"We'll switch in a bit," Bullard said. "Surprisingly, I'm doing okay yet, but I'll let you take her down."

"Yeah, it's still a long flight," Ryland said studying the islands below. It was a stunning view of the area.

"I love the islands here. Sometimes I just wonder about the benefit of, you know, crashing into the sea, coming up on a deserted island, and finding the simple life again," Bullard said with a laugh.

"I hear you," Ryland said. "Every once in a while, I wonder the same."

Several hours later Ryland looked up and said abruptly, "We've made good time considering we've already passed Fiji."

Bullard yawned.

"Let's switch."

Bullard smiled, nodded, and said, "Fine. I'll hand it over to you."

Just then a funny noise came from the engine on the right side.

They looked at each other, and Ryland said, "Uh-oh. That's not good news."

Boom!

And the plane exploded.

Find Bullard's Battle (Book #1) here!

To find out more visit Dale Mayer's website.

smarturl.it/DMSRyland

Damon's Deal: Terkel's Team (Book #1)

Welcome to a brand-new connected series of intrigue, betrayal, and ... murder, from the *USA Today* best-selling author Dale Mayer. A series with all the elements you've come to love, plus so much more... including psychics!

A betrayal from within has Terkel frantic to protect those he can, as his team falls one by one, from a murderous killer he helped create.

ICE POURED HERSELF a coffee and sat down at the compound's massive dining room table with the others. When her phone rang, she smiled at the number displayed. "Hey, Terk. How're you doing?" She put the call on Speakerphone.

"I'm okay," Terkel said, his voice distracted and tight.

"Terk?" Merk called from across the table. He got up and walked closer and sat across from Levi. "You don't sound too good, brother. What's up?"

"I'm fine," Terk said. "Or I will be. Right now, things are blown to shit."

"As in literally?" Merk asked.

"The entire group," Terk said, "they're all gone. I had a solid team of eight, and they're all gone."

"Dead?"

Several others stood to join them, gathered around Ice's phone. Levi stepped forward, his hand on Ice's shoulder. "Terk? Are they all dead?"

"No." Terk took a deep breath. "I'm not making sense. I'm sorry."

"Take it easy," Ice said, her voice calm and reassuring. "What do you mean, *they're all gone*?"

"All their abilities are gone," he said. "Something's happened to them. Somebody has deliberately removed whatever super senses they could utilize—or what we have been utilizing for the last ten years for the government." His tone was bitter. "When the US gov recently closed us down, they promised that our black ops department would never rise again, but I didn't expect them to attack us personally."

"What are you talking about?" Merk said in alarm, standing up now to stare at Ice's phone. "Are you in danger?"

"Maybe? I don't know," Terk said. "I need to find out exactly what the hell's going on."

"What can we do to help?" Ice asked.

Terk gave a broken laugh. "That's not why I'm calling. Well, it is, but it isn't."

Ice looked at Merk, who frowned, as he shook his head. Ice knew he and the others had heard Terk's stressed out tone and the completely confusing bits and pieces coming from his mouth. Ice said, "Terk, you're not making sense again. Take a breath and explain. Please. You're scaring me."

Terk took a long slow deep breath. "Tell Stone to open the gate," he said. "She's out there."

"Who's out there?" Levi asked, hopped up, looked outside, and shrugged.

"She's coming up the road now. You have to let her in."

"Who? Why?"

"*Because*," he said, "she's also harnessed with C-4."

"Jesus," Levi said, bolting to display the camera feeds to the big screen in the room. "Is it live?"

"It is, and she's been sent to you."

"Well, that's an interesting move," Ice said, her voice sharp, activating her comm to connect to Stone in the control room. "Who's after us?"

"I think it's rebels within the Iranian government. But it could be our own government. I don't know anymore," Terk snapped. "I also don't know how they got her so close to you. Or how they pinned your connection to me," he said. "I've been very careful."

"We can look after ourselves," Ice said immediately. "But who is this woman to you?"

"She's pregnant," he said, "so that adds to the intensity here."

"Understood. So who is the father? Is he connected somehow?"

There was silence on the other end.

Merk said, "Terk, talk to us."

"She's carrying my baby," Terk replied, his voice heavy.

Merk, his expression grim, looked at Ice, her face mirroring his shock. He asked, "How do you know her, Terk?"

"Brother, you don't understand," Terk said. "I've never met this woman before in my life." And, with that, the phone went dead.

Find Terkel's Team (Book #1) here!

To find out more visit Dale Mayer's website.

smarturl.it/DMSTTDamon

Author's Note

Thank you for reading North's Nikki: Heroes for Hire, Book 15! If you enjoyed the book, please take a moment and leave a short review.

Dear reader,

I love to hear from readers, and you can contact me at my website: www.dalemayer.com or at my Facebook author page. To be informed of new releases and special offers, sign up for my newsletter or follow me on BookBub. And if you are interested in joining Dale Mayer's Reader Group, here is the Facebook sign up page.
https://smarturl.it/DaleMayerFBGroup

Cheers,
Dale Mayer

Your THREE Free Books Are Waiting!

Grab your copy of SEALs of Honor Books 1 – 3 for free!

Meet Mason, Hawk and Dane. *Brave, badass warriors who serve their country with honor and love their women to the limits of life and death.*

DOWNLOAD your copy right now! Just tell me where to send it.

www.smarturl.it/DaleHonorFreeBundle

About the Author

Dale Mayer is a *USA Today* best-selling author, best known for her SEALs military romances, her Psychic Visions series, and her Lovely Lethal Garden cozy series. Her contemporary romances are raw and full of passion and emotion (Broken But ... Mending series). Her thrillers will keep you guessing (By Death series), and her romantic comedies will keep you giggling (*It's a Dog's Life*, a stand-alone novella; and the Broken Protocols series, starring Charming Marvin, the cat).

Dale honors the stories that come to her—and some of them are crazy and break all the rules and cross multiple genres!

To go with her fiction, she also writes nonfiction in many different fields, with books available on résumé writing, companion gardening, and the US mortgage system. She has recently published her Career Essentials series. All her books are available in print and ebook format.

Connect with Dale Mayer Online

Dale's Website – www.dalemayer.com
Twitter – @DaleMayer
Facebook – facebook.com/DaleMayer.author
BookBub – bookbub.com/authors/dale-mayer

Also by Dale Mayer

Published Adult Books:

Bullard's Battle

Ryland's Reach, Book 1

Cain's Cross, Book 2

Eton's Escape, Book 3

Garret's Gambit, Book 4

Kano's Keep, Book 5

Fallon's Flaw, Book 6

Quinn's Quest, Book 7

Bullard's Beauty, Book 8

Bullard's Best, Book 9

Terkel's Team

Damon's Deal, Book 1

Kate Morgan

Simon Says… Hide, Book 1

Hathaway House

Aaron, Book 1

Brock, Book 2

Cole, Book 3

Denton, Book 4

The K9 Files

Psychic Vision Series

Tuesday's Child

Hide 'n Go Seek

Maddy's Floor

Garden of Sorrow

Knock Knock...

Rare Find

Eyes to the Soul

Now You See Her

Shattered

Into the Abyss

Seeds of Malice

Eye of the Falcon

Itsy-Bitsy Spider

Unmasked

Deep Beneath

From the Ashes

Stroke of Death

Ice Maiden

Snap, Crackle...

Psychic Visions Books 1–3

Psychic Visions Books 4–6

Psychic Visions Books 7–9

By Death Series

Touched by Death

Haunted by Death

Chilled by Death

By Death Books 1–3

Broken Protocols – Romantic Comedy Series

Cat's Meow

Cat's Pajamas

Cat's Cradle

Cat's Claus

Broken Protocols 1-4

Broken and... Mending

Skin

Scars

Scales (of Justice)

Broken but... Mending 1-3

Glory

Genesis

Tori

Celeste

Glory Trilogy

Biker Blues

Morgan: Biker Blues, Volume 1

Cash: Biker Blues, Volume 2

SEALs of Honor

Mason: SEALs of Honor, Book 1

Hawk: SEALs of Honor, Book 2

Dane: SEALs of Honor, Book 3

Swede: SEALs of Honor, Book 4

Shadow: SEALs of Honor, Book 5

Cooper: SEALs of Honor, Book 6

Heroes for Hire

Heroes for Hire, Books 10–12
Heroes for Hire, Books 13–15

SEALs of Steel
Badger: SEALs of Steel, Book 1
Erick: SEALs of Steel, Book 2
Cade: SEALs of Steel, Book 3
Talon: SEALs of Steel, Book 4
Laszlo: SEALs of Steel, Book 5
Geir: SEALs of Steel, Book 6
Jager: SEALs of Steel, Book 7
The Final Reveal: SEALs of Steel, Book 8
SEALs of Steel, Books 1–4
SEALs of Steel, Books 5–8
SEALs of Steel, Books 1–8

The Mavericks
Kerrick, Book 1
Griffin, Book 2
Jax, Book 3
Beau, Book 4
Asher, Book 5
Ryker, Book 6
Miles, Book 7
Nico, Book 8
Keane, Book 9
Lennox, Book 10
Gavin, Book 11
Shane, Book 12

Diesel, Book 13

Jerricho, Book 14

The Mavericks, Books 1–2

The Mavericks, Books 3–4

The Mavericks, Books 5–6

The Mavericks, Books 7–8

The Mavericks, Books 9–10

The Mavericks, Books 11–12

Collections

Dare to Be You…

Dare to Love…

Dare to be Strong…

RomanceX3

Standalone Novellas

It's a Dog's Life

Riana's Revenge

Second Chances

Published Young Adult Books:

Family Blood Ties Series

Vampire in Denial

Vampire in Distress

Vampire in Design

Vampire in Deceit

Vampire in Defiance

Vampire in Conflict

Vampire in Chaos

Vampire in Crisis

Vampire in Control

Vampire in Charge

Family Blood Ties Set 1–3

Family Blood Ties Set 1–5

Family Blood Ties Set 4–6

Family Blood Ties Set 7–9

Sian's Solution, A Family Blood Ties Series Prequel Novelette

Design series

Dangerous Designs

Deadly Designs

Darkest Designs

Design Series Trilogy

Standalone

In Cassie's Corner

Gem Stone (a Gemma Stone Mystery)

Time Thieves

Published Non-Fiction Books:

Career Essentials

Career Essentials: The Résumé

Career Essentials: The Cover Letter

Career Essentials: The Interview

Career Essentials: 3 in 1

Made in United States
Orlando, FL
22 May 2022

18088261R00133